Praise for *The Shutter of Snow*

"An extraordinary, visionary book, written out of those edges where madness and poetry meet."—Fay Weldon

"*The Shutter of Snow* is a profoundly moving book, supplying as it does a glimpse of what a temporary derangement and its consequences may mean to the sufferer."—*The Nation*

"Seldom does one of Mrs. Coleman's background become a victim of psychosis and come back to tell the tale. Certainly there has never been a book containing such a vivid experience in the field of mental shadow as she remembers."—*Boston Transcript*

"Mrs. Coleman has succeeded in conveying the pity and terror of the condition in a remarkable manner, without exaggeration and without self-pity or sentimentality. It is a success very rarely achieved in any kind of literature."—*The Nation and Athenæum* (London)

"The crisp wit which delighted Mrs. Coleman's examiners even when she was psychopathic saves her book from being too utterly depressing. The story of daily life in a ward for the insane is not likely to be merry reading, nor does Mrs. Coleman desire it to be; her intent has an obvious depth beyond that, but there are abysses into which it is hardly fair to lead a reader under the guise of the novel. *The Shutter of Snow* avoids these without being false to its essential tragedy."—*Saturday Review of Literature*

"A very striking triumph of imagination and technique. . . . The book is not only unique; it is also a work of genuine literary inspiration."—Edwin Muir

the Shutter of Snow
Emily Holmes Coleman

Dalkey Archive

Originally published in 1930 by George Routledge & Sons
Limited (New York).
© 1930 by Emily Holmes Coleman.
Copyright renewed 1974 by the Estate of Emily Holmes Coleman.
All rights reserved

First Dalkey Archive Edition, 1997.

Coleman, Emily Holmes, 1899-1974.
The shutter of snow / Emily Holmes Coleman. — 1st Dalkey
Archive ed.
p.   cm.
ISBN 1-56478-147-X
I. Title.
PS3505.02783S58   1997   813'.52—dc21   96-51794

This publication is supported by grants from the National
Endowment for the Arts, a federal agency, and the Illinois Arts
Council, a state agency.

Dalkey Archive Press
Illinois State University
Campus Box 4241
Normal, IL 61790-4241

*Printed on permanent/durable acid-free paper and bound in the
United States of America.*

the Shutter of Snow

I

There were two voices that were louder than the others. At night when the red light was out in the hall and there was someone sitting in a chair in front of the door clearing her throat at intervals there would be the voices far down the hall mingling with sobs and shouts and the drones of those who were beginning to sleep. It was cold and she shivered under the blankets. She cried out that she was cold and the woman came in and took a blanket out and warmed it for her. Then she would be wrapped in the hot blanket very tightly and the covers tucked in over that. My feet are cold. Her throat was always hot, like old bread in the sun. Her lips stood out and were cracked and there was water gushing on the other side of the wall. There was chicken wire up over her door.

The window was closed and the bars went up and down on the outside. She could hear the wind sliding the snow off the roof. An avalanche of snow gathered and fell and buried the sun beneath. There were six bars to the back of her bed.

The voices were carrying stones from one field to another. They dropped the stones and other voices picked them up and threw them into a loose-planked wagon. One of them came from the other side of her bed, the other side of that wall. There was nothing in the room but the bed and the chicken wire and high up on the wall the iron grating where she threw the plates. There was no light in the room. Only a dull red light in the hall. Someone was walking back and forth back and forth passing her door a captive. The voice on the other side of her wall was shouting for someone. It never stopped all night. It became entangled in the blankets and whistled the ice prongs on the wind. The rest of the voices were not so distinct. It was very still out in the hall when the voices stopped.

She called and said she wanted water. The woman brought her a round thick white cup. But its never enough my throat is so dry. If you would stop talking your throat wouldnt be like that.

She had to say it all and when it was said and when every word had been sealed into the night wind's casket, she would stop. She had been a foetus and had knitted herself together in the bed. Then she had come noiselessly forth and they had fed her. The sunny morning and Hazel feeding her out of a bowl. Clean cheeks and a little river in her teeth. Pine needles dripping in the Caucasus.

Her father had come in the door and she had cried to him. All of them standing around her bed, not this bed, pointing to the baby and to the wall. She had thrown the medicine glass at the wall and made a livid spot in it. They took away her little baby. The top of his head was soft and sunken. Down with her chin in the silk and sunk, and flowing up around her cheeks the dying. She had warmed him in her bed.

She got up from the blankets and gathered them round her and struggled out into the hall. The red lights were boring into her eyes, sharp and returning. What are you doing out of bed? I want to go to the bathroom. The woman helped her into the bathroom. When she came to the door she saw a groaning skeleton with wisps of hair and great yellow teeth, rubbing her hands on her nightgown. Her face was a lion coming forth to kill. Marthe put out her hand and drew back with a sharp scream. She screamed into her hands and tore at the woman's apron. She fled back to her room, the blanket dragging behind her cold feet. Whats the matter you arent afraid of that poor old lady are you? The skeleton was coming into her room. She came slowly in, larger and larger. She approached the bed, chewing her horrid hands.

Marthe was cold and her throat made no sound. You must not be afraid, remember who you are. She sat up in the bed and fastened her eyes on the skeleton. She pointed her finger towards the door. She stared through her, the pupils of her eyes came out and went into her and through her and came out behind her. Her eyes opened and covered her whole face, and her teeth were closed. The skeleton went out.

Marthe sank back into the bed. I can do it I must always remember I can do it. Godwin was wrapping her in another blanket. Now mind you dont get out of bed again, she said, or youll catch it. Is she gone? Who? That person. You mean poor old Miss Ryan? Shes gone back to her bed. She cried on Godwin's uniform. She felt her wedding ring. They took my wedding ring, she said. I dont know where it is. How long do you think it will be before I can see him? Tomorrow perhaps. It was always tomorrow. They all said tomorrow, no matter what the question was. You will have to learn to sleep before you can see him.

How could they expect her to sleep when she was going through all of it? They didnt know. She had swung about the room from the ceiling and it was a swinging from the cross. There had been the burial. She was lying quietly in the bed and being covered over her face. She was carried quietly out and put in the casket. Down, down she went in the rectangle that had been made for her. Down and the dirt fell in above. Down and the worms began to tremble in and out. Always she had kept telling of it, not one word of it must be forgotten. It must all be recorded in sound and after that she could sleep.

She must recall everything. When the last itemized syllable was told it would all be over. No one would understand until that had happened and at that moment all the graves would be flung open and all the lovers would love.

They didnt understand now. They laughed and were hard. They filed past like moving picture actresses, with trays, their lips well reddened and laughing.

She tore from her tender skin the rough nightgown. She jumped out from the bed into the warm and heavy hall. She stampeded the big door, the door that led outside. I will go out of here, why am I here? She pounded with her fists on the door. It has come, the hour has come. We are all to be free. A voice shouted break it down break it down. All the beds in the back began to shout. Godwin rushed to hold her wrists to twist them. She shook her off like autumn leaves. Godwin rattled and fell away. She struck Godwin in the face and looked savagely about for more resistance.

The door broke from the other side and she was surrounded. They twisted both her wrists and she was calm. It was the first pain she had had. She had thought pain was gone with the rest. My husband, she cried to Miss Sheehan, why cant I see him? She was being wound up like a French doll. She could not move. If she moved a finger two of them began to twist her wrists. The others wound the strips of cloth together. Miss Sheehan, how can you betray me like this? When it was done they carried her like a stone Pharaoh to her bed. She was put into bed with the blankets and over that the canvas sheet was pulled. It was very strong and thick with a hole for the head. But I cant sleep on my back.

They went on talking noisily. My, shes a strong one, who would ever think it to look at her? They were rubbing their hands together loosely when it was done.

In the bed and from the bed there was only the hall in the daytime. There were the actresses who walked past rehearsing their parts, rouged and strong. She saw through it quickly enough and wished they would think of harder things to do. The same ones would go back in halves and then in quarters and she could always remember the legs.

At first the keys were chimes that glistened in crooked inter-vals. They clinged into and through and past. Cling, push, through, shut and past. She lay in the bed and fastened her gaze on the crack of her door. The keys glittered through and swung from the middle. They went always past. When her door was closed she would wait for that key. She waited for sixteen days counting the minutes and the clingpushthroughshut and past.

The keys jangled from the waists of the nurses. They rattled like silver dishpans and swung chanting high like death songs. They were brittle and ice cold and had faces of stagnant riders from the snow. They were proud, and deliciously ate their in-difference.

Yahweh had to be damned and she must never stop. He was often in the iron grating high above her bed and she shook screaming fists and condemned him. There would be no more interference from Yahweh, that at least would be her contribu-tion. It was too much that houses should fall on bright slant eyes in the cherry blossoms, and that he should sit up there in the grating, removed and merciful.

Little Mary Soulier was in the room. She had been one of the voices. She sat in the stiff chair and shook her hair and her eyes shut with laughter. She had had five puppies and they all had died. They wept the puppies in unison. Marthe swung up her legs and turned to Mary in a gathering whirlwind. She held tight her ankles, and her legs and arms and hands wept with her neck. She turned to the opposite wall and poured forth in bitterness and weeping. Christopher, Christopher was in the ground with never a touch of her lips to his hand. Never would he speed up the hill to touch the feet of the lark before it flew. My beautiful, my calm head. The baby was with him hidden close in the grave clothes. The little white baby with quiet eyes that would not take of her milk. They wept together and Marthe had wept all her tears. There were no more tears and she wept with clean stark eyes.

That afternoon there was a great chair out in the hall and Yahweh was sitting in it. He was reading her small green Shelley and she had not given it to him. You take what you see and call it good but it is not good. He sat in the chair and read in a speckled bathrobe and had wads of hair over each ear. His eyes started out and came back.

Mary Soulier was French and was teaching her to sing. Marthe's mind was new, it was bright like tall razors. Her fine new mind green and cutting. Are the babies all damned if they arent baptized? No of course not, that isnt the way they do, they love the babies. I will change that, there shall be no more of that. They damned my puppies said Mary. She had falling black hair and a great smile. Her eyes swam in it. She moved with grace of snake coming up a tree. She danced in Marthe's room and sang French songs. You will not be a voice any more? No I shall strangle all the voices if they keep you awake.

II

Marthe was sitting up in bed winding rags. Mary sat opposite telling her what each rag was. There was a small one shorter than all the others. Mary made a ring of it and put it on Marthe's finger. That is the shortest one, Jesus wept. You must always wear that to remember. I have been in the post office said Mary, and there is nothing to be done about it nothing at all. The only thing to do is to put hammers in the porridge and when there are enough hammers we shall break down the windows and all of us shall dance in the snow.

All of us shall dance in the snow.

Mary had been beautiful the night in the bath. Shapes, all of them grotesque, the female body. All of them with breasts that did not fit, and rotting elbows. Toenails and trailing hair. She had looked away and had stood trembling slipping the towel. She had sunk into the great tub and swum out her legs in warm lilies. The gurgling water came around her and lengthened her body in mud. Mary with calm lovely face looking at her from the demons that stood around with inept towels. And after that, it was a long time after, Mary had been in the other bathroom in the tub with wide sheet across. She had been a head a lovely dead head floating above the canvas sheet and Marthe had taken the broom to crush her head. I shall have no more death you are a corpse a beautiful one but I am not afraid. Mary had smiled above the tub. I am not dirty they are all dirty except Mary and me. Pick up that thread youll have to learn to pick up every thread or you will never get out of here.

The bed was moved over to the gray window. Through the bars the distance and on the ground the snow. Bits of orange peel in the snow but she could not see the nightgowns. She had thrown them all there, she had pushed them out through the bars.

Outside of the window was an evergreen tree. There were hundreds of sparrows in it. When she was God they clustered in the tree, when the pillow was on the bed and she was God. When the pillow was on the floor they flew a thousand ways and wept their wings. On the other side of the tree was a long cement walk and the edge of a brick building and there were lights all over that. There was a fire escape at the end. The lights came on when it was night and came on again in the early morning. She never saw any people in the lights.

To the left was a low building and she did not know what it was. There were two horses and a wagon standing by it and the man threw boxes from the wagon. She did not know where this was. It wasnt the Gorestown State Hospital. She knew that was to fool her, she could see through these stupidities. They didnt know her mind was new and brilliantly lighted. G S H on all the sheets and blankets. They had not forgotten one. They were clever these people but she knew. When she had passed every test there would be the opening of the graves. She strained her eyes but never could see beyond this. It was a dark day and the snow had slunk under the cellars. Her father must be taken care of first. He was the one Yahweh had trifled with. She would make him smile his whistling smile, he would whistle for her bright in the new morning, whistle the Mill Song and strop his razor. She loved his hands and his cuffs on which he had written the name of every lamb. She had named all the lambs and he had remembered them. She would make him a blue handkerchief with a great J which would be like life springs to him. He would vault over the great gate with one hand and when the bull charged on the tree he would spring to one side. Her father, with chocolate almonds in the hay.

III

Mrs Welsh is going to pray with me. We are going to pray together because she believes. She was close to the ground and had round hair and a sloughing body. She had one tooth out and always carried her prayer book. The priest says I am a devil. Mrs Welsh popped herself into the room and sat on the bed in her checked dress. The prayer book was closed. Did you hear how that woman upstairs hid marmalade under the mattress for two weeks and the nurses only just found it? What woman? Shes upstairs, you havent seen her. Whats upstairs? Why the quiet ones. Youll get there some day. Ive been there often. Why are you here now then? I had a row with Dr Armitage. I came right out in the hall and yelled out in front of everybody what he was. What does he look like? He comes in here often, dont let him fool you, dont speak to him. I'll remember. What else? Well I saw stars, Ive had four children you know. Mrs Welsh shook herself and went to the window. You are lucky to have a private room.

Mrs Welsh returned to the bed and opened her prayer book. Marthe read the litany. Her voice sank into it and made of it a golden cup with ragged lily edges. I always used to hate it, she said, I wouldnt say I was a miserable sinner, and got into trouble all the time. Mrs Welsh threw back her head and the gap showed in her teeth.

They continued with the litany. Marthe's voice staggered, the little bones in her neck protruded. Mrs Welsh watched with tears dropping down. Its lovely. You see said Marthe, Im going to tell you because you are the only one who isnt a damn fool. I am Jesus Christ she said. This time its a woman she said quietly. I dont expect you to believe it.

Mrs Welsh was grave and her eyes were stiff at attention. I do believe she said. It was a call from God I had she said, that day I was ironing. When you were singing? Yes and you came running in crying. I loved your voice she said, Mrs Welsh you have a beautiful voice. You remember how you were crying and running away from the nurse? Yes I knew she was going to put me in the sheet. I heard you singing and I ran in. You grabbed me and begged me to find your husband said Mrs Welsh wiping her eyes. Theres no use crying, she said. But why do you want your husband, Im well rid of mine. I dont know said Marthe. Does your husband know youre here? said Mrs Welsh. No, and they wont tell him.

Mrs Welsh knelt down on the floor and took up her beads. I had to laugh she explained first. That Miss Andrews, the one thats sweet on the janitor, has paint all over her dress. How? From fooling with him I suppose said Mrs Welsh, hes painting the back hall. Whats back of that door? Its the Day Room, when you get better you can go out there. What do they do there? They sew in the afternoon. O do you suppose they would let me sew? Let you said Mrs Welsh, theyll make you.

O all ye flowers and winds bless ye the Lord praise him and magnify him forever. O all ye seas and floods bless ye the Lord praise him and magnify him forever. O let the earth bless the Lord yea let it praise him and magnify him forever.

Mary came deftly in and sat down on the edge of the bed. She was holding a doll. It was a towel and a ribbon. Marthe cried give him to me its my baby. Mary was beautiful. Marthe remembered her head bobbing like a dead apple above the water. Give him to me hes mine. He is not yours said Mary, I made this baby and its mine. Whats mine is mine and is not yours. She looked out calmly. Yes said Mrs Welsh, you must remember. Marthe sat back. I cannot have my baby she said.

The first time she came into the hall after she could feed herself someone was shouting numbers in a football game. Mrs Fearing was wandering up and down in her gray wrapper making faces as she counted. I dont understand said Marthe. I am going to kill you said Mrs Fearing and laughed disgustingly. Marthe cried out and ran into her room. Shes coming after me. Youre not very brave are you said the nurse. Marthe came out again and stood in the hall to look. The great door opened to let in the trays and they marched past with stiff shoulders. The red lights were on. O you have a pencil said Marthe, please can I have it? Mrs Fearing had a red face and blood on her nose. Please give me the pencil? No. I need one very much I want to write a letter. No said Mrs Fearing and retreated with the pencil. Marthe reached out to take it and Mrs Fearing made a guttural shout and plunged her finger nails into her hair. Marthe struck out at her. Shes killing me Mrs Fearing cried. You will have the sheet for that said the nurse to Mrs Fearing. Marthe's head throbbed. She picked up the pencil. It wasnt her fault, I tried to get the pencil. Mrs Fearing was led back to her room.

Marthe sat down in the hall. They said she could eat her supper in the hall. She held tightly to the pencil. She could write now, she could write two letters. They would know about it now because she would write. Her father and Christopher would know and they would come on winded wings to take her away. The nurse gave her a small piece of paper. Eat your supper she said.

Marthe very quickly ate up her mush and the prunes. She ate every little drop. She was going to write a letter.

She sat at the big table in the hall, the bare white wood table with the dirty trays. She folded the piece of paper and tore it precisely in two. She held the pencil tightly and began to write words.

The words unfolded and came out on the paper. They slid up and floated and came down and stood in line. She was making them, she was saying things with a pencil on a small piece of yellow paper. It was a letter to her father and there were the words, the words that she was capturing out of the red lights and pinning under her pencil like squirming moths. The moths had yellow tails and pulled desperately away from the pencil.

That was done. There were the two letters. There would have to be envelopes and then there would be the addresses. She could remember the addresses well enough. She could write those too, and then the letters would go out and she would be free.

I'll get you the envelopes, said the nurse. It was Miss Sheehan. She took the letters and put them in a pocket. She walked Marthe around to the other beds. You can have a promenade she said, and then you must go to bed. They walked down the hall to the beds where the voices were.

Marthe shuddered from them into the nurse's shoulder. They are corpses she said. The skeleton was there and the other voices. They were all there, lying under the canvas sheets. One of them was a German voice. The red lights made them devils and their heads and arms were all she could see. Thin crunching arms and screaming fingers to the light. She was afraid and cried into the hall. I hate them and I am afraid of them. They are groping devils and their heads are wound with snow. They have lost their bodies, their bodies have melted away, she said. The little one has matted curls in the back and she is a wart on her bed. I never want to see them again, she cried to Miss Sheehan, they are dead devils.

This was Dr Brainerd. Of course you remember her, said Mrs Welsh, youve seen her every day. You must be quiet when she comes in. Dr Brainerd was a hearty strong voice and laugh. Her voice was low when she looked away to say something and louder when she looked back. Her face was handsome, brown glasses and brown eyes. Her voice was like deep beds of sand by the side of a lake. You dont remember me? You told me I was a damn fool. She laughed and looked away. Would you like to see your husband? she said then. Marthe began to cry. Look out at that snow said the doctor, wouldnt you like to roll in it? I dont want to roll in the snow said Marthe.

I like your husband said Dr Brainerd, he is a clever young man. Dont talk about him said Marthe fiercely. She was ashamed. I suppose everybody cries when you come in she said. Indeed not said Dr Brainerd looking out of the window. You see she said, hes been coming every day but I didnt think it would be good for you to see him for a while. Would you like to see him today?

Today. It was a day and there was a morning outside. There would be red lights again in the evening. You will be very quiet?

Then he knows Im here, he has been coming every day and you wouldnt let him see me? Dr Brainerd turned away and went out the door.

He was coming today. It would be sometime before the red lights. He would come stalking in the door with his gentle hands and would smile at everything she said. He would look up from under his eyebrows and demand to know what she meant. He would have purple sandals and a crown of laurel. He would bring her a casket of roses and she would crush them on the floor. And there would be under his coat the little snow-haired baby with clenched hands.

Someone was coming into the room again after the keys rattled. It was the uncle who used to give her French dolls. Why Uncle Jim cried Marthe. She wept again. This is Dr Armitage said Dr Brainerd. When did you come said Marthe, you are going to take me out? No I want to see how you are.

Why does everybody try to fool me, dont you think this has lasted long enough? she cried clasping her fingers. She jumped out on the floor. Lets call this joke off she cried.

You must get back into bed, they both said, you are getting excited again. Im not excited she screamed, cant you see its because youre all so crazy? She threw out her arms and her voice penetrated the bars and drew out their metal marrow. They put her quietly in the bed. If you will promise to be quiet I wont have them put on the sheet said Dr Brainerd. I'll promise nothing she shouted. I hate you and I hate them all. Do you hear me Dr Brainerd? Dont stand there looking at me with your sorrowing voice. They put the sheet over her and the doctors went out.

IV

You see said Mrs Welsh, I told you not to have anything to do with Dr Armitage. But I tell you it wasnt Dr Armitage it was my own uncle and they have told him to pretend hes not, she shouted. They are playing this cruel game to fool me and I wont stand it another minute. Her arms were bound.

Be careful said Mrs Welsh. Dont yell so loud or youll never get upstairs. Hell hell I dont care, goddam, goddam, goddam everyone in this whole goddamned building. Goddam Jesus Mary and Joseph and every one of the whole goddamned family. Mrs Welsh opened startled eyes but nothing happened and the wind blew around the trees outside over the crusted snow.

Tell me about upstairs she said finally. Well said Mrs Welsh sitting back, you can have oranges and crackers in your room and you eat in the dining room. With forks? Yes and sometimes they go on sleigh rides. Is the snow very deep? Yes and the men are digging a path, I can see them from here. What men? The men on the other side. How big is this place? said Marthe, straining her eyes to see. About 1700 I guess said Mrs Welsh. My Lord God 1700 of them like this with lies and tricks and cruelty and no one to help them. Oh no said Mrs Welsh, the nurses here are very nice. My grandfather was in the asylum at Covington and it was something awful. Here theyre decent to you. Theyre not, theyre cruel, they do everything they can think of to make us more miserable.

Where is this place, do you know? Dont you know? said Mrs Welsh astonished. She pulled out a corner of the blanket from under the sheet. Do you mean to say you let them fool you with that? cried Marthe, thats just another one of their tricks. Why no said Mrs Welsh, didnt you get your commitment papers the first day? I dont remember the first day, I dont remember anything.

What do you think it is? said Mrs Welsh. I think its a bawdy house and theyre going to kill all of us if we dont kill them first. Can you untie that knot down there? I wouldnt dare said Mrs Welsh, now you be good and stay quiet. Look, here come the trays. I'll feed you.

What is it said Marthe, anything decent? Its macaroni and tomato and theres apple sauce. She put a slice of buttered bread in Marthe's mouth. Say, this ward isnt anything. Theres a ward in one of the other buildings where they have tin plates. I was in it said Mrs Welsh.

The lights grew dull red in the hall and Mrs Welsh went to her own bed. The night voices began to waver back and forth. She was leaning above the shed in the haymow and they were going to kill the steer. They said she couldnt see and she had climbed to see and it made her stomach jump. Posy was tucking her in and pumping her breasts with the small pump that hurt her breasts. Just a little bit more. They were taking the baby away after she had hidden him under the covers and warmed him with her body when his feet were cold. She had felt his feet under the little blanket. They found him and took him away and she pounded the doctor on the chest. And Christopher was lying on the outside of her bed on the counterpane, holding her tightly and talking to her. You must stop talking and go to sleep. No one can make me stop until I am through. She looked around the white room and was baked in clay. She hid the ugly little baby under the blankets and the nurses couldnt find him. She sang to him under the covers, under her breath, and kissed his calm head.

There was the ether again, it was floating above her head. Freshly her flamed face turned to it, the sweet sharp odour that had been release. She tasted delicately the soft descent into the flowers of tranquillity. She swam her legs out before her and her ears fell upon pond lilies. Christopher she called, I am going to die. He came in and saw her lying still with only her nose showing from the cloth. The ice melted down her ears.

Now there was peace in the white room. She lay on her side making white edges on her brittle nails and swinging in yards of green space. She swung out to the edge of a green cloud and back again to her bed. And as she swung she swooped down upon her nails. I must keep very quiet or she'll think Im sick. There was the red nurse and the one with the dogs in the French chateau. Posy was not there. The red one had emerald cheeks. The stitches were pulled out and she was swinging from them.

He had become acres tall. He leaned above the bed an elongated ribbon of ink. Reach down to me she cried. He squatted in the hard chair. I cant hear a word he says I want to swing again. Will you look? he said. Certainly I will look my dear one. She leaned across to see and wrinkled her forehead to see. Here he is chasing the man out. You see the dog is biting him. Thats the little boys behind the barrel. Yes I see. Here he is holding on to his leg and shaking his fist. Why does he shake his fist like a ruined father? The dog bit him dont you remember? But why in that one is the dog sitting with him? Cant you see its not the same man. If I get hold of youse kids I'll lay your heads together. What for Christopher? But darling you dont remember *anything.*

Come near to me you are so far away. She reached out with her oar and tried to poke him into her stream. Posy brought her the medicine and she threw the little glass at the wall. There remained a livid spot in the plaster and she looked into it and all her life went mingling in concentric circles in the green spot. She and Christopher and the baby went into shifts and coils and clouds, round and round in the spot.

There he was her father, he came in the door and she didnt know he was coming. She gave a loud cry to him. He was very tall and he breathed the stream where they had made the dam at the Devil's Hole. There was a great green slope and she had pricked her bare feet in the creek. There was the dam he had built and there were the lambs she had named. And over it all was the tearless one who had left him when he was happy and gone into brown fields without him. It was this that was to be again, he was to have this again and in his heart was growing a stern and ruddy pear that he would take and offer for them both. He would make of his heart a stolen marrow bone and clutch snow crystals in the night to his liking. He came by her bed and she told into his hand the whole of what it had been. She knows him they said, and they stood around the bed and she told them what they must do.

And she rustled in and out in a carcass of black silk, that was her mother and her father would never see her again. Now she knew what had happened now she could see. It had been this it had been this very thing, and he was to stand it a second time. Her mother had rustled in and out of the silk and bars and had whispered into her coffin. And he had seen her lying still there on the floor and had cried out to the doctors that she was very well and could not be dead. They saw him weep in his granite tower and the shaking stream poured down the battlements of his tower and melted to soft poppies in the rain of his annulment. He had gone crying in the flood of his bewilderment and now it was she who came creeping to him from his new and iron courage, and when the morning of his sorrow had come there she was holding to the stump of her freedom and pushing his hands away. But when the brown canvas straps rolled down, down, and into the deepness of the eternal earth his love went silently, she held tightly his hand and his folded mouth was set to the acceptance. It all went down, it went forever from his face, and they walked away when tulips had been thrown to mark the place.

That was to her the infinity of comprehension and forever from that day she was to sing the Mill Song that she knew he would whistle. He was to whistle in the early morning and she was to set his candle on the chair and bring him stockings finely folded. Now the baby was crumpled into the red lights and the night voices called across the spaces of sleep.

V

That was the first time she saw the outside. The white nurse with the hollow eyes came in and nodded her head. There was a wheel chair and heavy blankets. She got into it carefully and the nurse wrapped her up. Where am I going? It was Mrs Wendy. She was a nurse, the head of all. Will you tell me just one thing, what did they do with my wedding ring? Its in the office in the safe said Mrs Wendy. But how did they get it? They took it off the first night you came when you were in the bath. But cant I have it now, Mrs Fearing has hers. Yours was loose Mrs Gail, I remember, it hung very loose on your finger.

The keys were for her now. They slipped around the ring and out and into the door. The great door swung out and she slid through in the chair. She was out and away and flying into new spaces. It was not fast like the cart in the hospital when all she could see was shooting lights above. It was gentle and she could look around. There was a large room with stiff cane chairs. Faces stared from all the walls, they had moon eyes and stared with them. Mrs Welsh had told her not to try to get away out there. Itll be worse for you if you do, stay right in the chair. She remembered the room now and the desk in the corner. I went through here the first night in a chair. Mrs Wendy nodded her cap. Yes you remember. I called them all damn fools she said. Where is my husband, is he out here? No not this time said Mrs Wendy. It would not be again.

It was brilliantly exciting to her fingers. They passed through and down a corridor. There were ferns and tables, there was a piano. An old straight lady with high white hair sat striking at the keys. Good morning Mrs Wendy, she said brightly and slid her hands across the black notes. They are not supposed to play before five o'clock.

The keys swung out on the chain and into and through this door. A dark hall, with doors on both sides. Down beyond that, down and through the door ahead. Another hall, brightly lighted, and a long green billiard table. Two men were walking around the table with sticks. They walked separately and in mixed steps. Down past that and a man was sitting on a bench outside a door. His face was torn and his eyes bulged inwardly to his head. His mouth hung in sorrow and his hands were gray. He is very unhappy said Marthe. They are all unhappy said Mrs Wendy. She smiled and nodded and her cap bobbed on her head.

They passed the man, who stared at them with bent eyebrows. The keys again and they did not fit. She knocked on the door and it came open from the other side, flooding them with white. The chair passed in silently.

A great whiteness like a purified star. Bottles and steel and white enamel legs. White padding and curious colours of fluids. Great white wheels encased in rubber. This is the operating room said Mrs Wendy. Now I know they are going to kill me, after all I know now, and she is here to cover it.

A young girl was telephoning at the desk. She was normally dressed. Marthe looked at her clothes. Her hair was in neat waves at the top of her head. Who is that? The girl laughed a boyish sound. That is Dr Halloway. Marthe stared at the young girl, her own age, dressed harmoniously, and telephoning.

Now all you have to do is bend over. A small patient man in a white coat. Then she was not going on the table, they were not going to kill her that way. She touched Mrs Wendy's fingers. They lifted her on to a stool and lifted her nightgown in the back. Bend over, this wont hurt. I wont make a sound whatever they do. A fork jammed into her spinal column and she stiffened in the air.

Its all done now, let me have your arm a minute. What was that? That was the Wassermann test, do you know what that is? Now she knew, they all had syphilis, that was what she had, they had given it to her when she was asleep. The three people in the room laughed because her face was drawn into horror. Every patient who comes in here has this done, very few of them have a positive reaction, they said.

A pump squeezed her arm and it was pricked for a blood test. The doctor smeared a piece of court plaster on her arm and another one on the base of her spine. Goodbye Mrs Gail. He shook hands with her. Dr Halloway came from behind the desk and shook hands with her. You will go home soon she said. My husband! cried Marthe. Is he the redheaded one? said Dr Halloway. Yes, yes, yes, thats he, do you know him, when am I going to see him, is he here?

He comes up here every day said Dr Halloway, havent you seen him? No, O no! she cried wringing her hands. You are going now they said.

She stared at the shining room white with sunlight. Cant I stay here a little while? Im sorry, said Dr Halloway, but this room is busy all the time. We had an operation for appendicitis here this morning and we're expecting a delivery tonight.

She was wheeled back, past the man, past the billiard table, down the dark hall, past the piano and into the Day Room. Cant I stay in the Day Room? she begged, just to look at that flower pot? I will be good, O I will be good.

Mrs Wendy reached out the key of the great door. Not this time she said, but youll be out here soon. O do I have to go back? Just for a short time she said.

She looked with all her body and eyes at the stiff chairs, the frowning eyes in the chairs, the windows on the snow, the desk in the corner with a white nurse sitting. There was a plant on the table with green leaves and shell pink flowers with red centres. Whose is that plant? she said as the door swung open. It closed heavily behind her.

She was in bed and her spine throbbed. She was wound up in a sheet. This is not because you were excited explained Miss Harrison. You mustnt move after this test. She was wound tightly and strapped into the canvas sheet. You cannot move until tomorrow afternoon, it may be painful. Her spine jabbed into her back with pitchfork tines but she lay still and looked at the ceiling. That didnt matter, nothing mattered after the other. Pain was nothing now and she didnt care. She looked at the window and began to sing. Her throat was sore and the singing came out like the sound of a motor boat. I can never sing again.

Mary had some picture books. What are those books? They are for my children. I didnt know you had any children said Marthe. Ive had three said Mary. They are all dead now she said, they have soft wings.

The most miserable one of all was Sarah Kemp. From the earliest days she was pacing up and down outside and crying. She had been Russia waiting for the Revolution, and after that she had been Marthe's mother, moaning alone and shut away. That was for her to know, to see, to teach her what her father had known. That was her mother, walking alone and her children gone. She grew older as she paced the hall and her hair that had been soft brown became spotted with gray. Marthe knew what her end would be, that she did not know. She would lie still in a strange room and it would be that she had broken her veins.

Mrs Kemp had a badly used face. Her hair was pulled back from a red and uncomprehending forehead. Her mouth fell into her chin. She marched up and down the hall. Now she was no longer a symbol, she was a cello accompaniment to a dirge. She came like a tiger thieving and walked away from the theft. She came like a panther back and forth, raising a head at the end of the bars.

Marthe lay in bed. She was God and could not get Mrs Kemp out of it. There were the red lights on now and always she was passing before them. All at once she turned and came into Marthe's room.

Listen my dear little girl, for the love of Jesus Mary and Joseph cant you get me out of this? Omygodmygod will I never get out of this? Her hands held in her forehead. She walked to the window and back to the door. Please go out of my room. She will try to kill me.

Have you no pity, look at me a fine woman like me in this hellhole, cant you do something about it? She leaned close to Marthe and put her hand on her shoulder. Marthe sat up in bed and fastened her eyes on the woman. She pointed her arm out towards the door. Do you hear me? Go out of here. She began to look into her shifting eyes.

Mrs Kemp backed away. She looked about, and turned and walked out of the room. She did not go by the door again that night. Marthe heard her moaning down the hall. She would pace as far as Marthe's door and then back again, but she did not pass the door. Marthe turned quietly to the wall and snuggled down under the blankets. It was cold it was always cold. They warmed blankets on the radiator for her at the end of the ward but she was always cold. Her feet were stiff every night. She wanted her warm slippers lined with sheep's wool.

She was never afraid of Mrs Kemp again. Why do you make such a fuss? You are no worse off than the rest of us. Oh yes said Miss Brunmark, the nurse with the jaunty hips and square dark eyes. Sarahs worse off than anybody in the world. Mrs Kemp paused in her walk. You see Mrs Gail she knows that Sarah Kemp is the most unhappy woman in the world. And talks the most about it, they said.

Why dont you stop that noise Mrs Kemp? nobody can sleep with you going on that way. Listen darling how can I stop when my Tims away from me and doesnt know Im here and they slipped it over on me and he cant get me out of this.

But Im in the same boat said Marthe. My husband doesnt know Im here either and they wont tell him. Then youre unhappy too poor dear said Mrs Kemp. She went on moaning. But we all are said Marthe. Why dont you shut up so we can sleep? She saw her pace down to the other end of the corridor and back up again. Why dont you commit suicide if youre so miserable? Mrs Kemp stood still and began to scream. She tore at her hair and threw her arms about. Will I never get out of this? She beat her head gently against the hot water pipe. Harder said Marthe, why dont you really hurt yourself?

She wouldnt hurt herself said Miss Brunmark, not her. She thinks too much of herself. Did she ever really try? I should say not, not that one said Brunmark. She did try once said Mary. She tried to jump down the laundry chute and you just got there in time. Yes and she tried to pretend she was drowning in the tub said Brunmark. Shes just a great big fake that one is. She dont get any sympathy out of me. And you listen to me, you arent to start yelling like that again or youll get the sheet.

Sarah Kemp looked at the nurse. She began to walk again.

VI

She was lying frailly in the bed, turned to the wall and making great circles on the wall with her eyes. They were life circles and it was her life. It would all be over now.

Hes coming now they said, is it the redheaded one? I saw him in the office. Hes coming now.

Her veins ran coldly in her arms. Her face was very hot. She was lying with her arms bound behind her back in the spiralled casket with the canvas sheet over all. There were many steps out in the hall. There had been her father who had whistled, and she had whistled back. She answered every time to let him know that she was there and knew him. But he had never come in, only slinking outside in the hall. They would not let him in.

Her door opened. It was Miss Harrison, her glasses shining. You will be quiet? I will be good, I will be very good.

He came in then. He had on rubbers and an old tie. His face was smaller. He walked slowly towards her and his eyes were gray. Why do you wear that tie when I threw it away?

He sat in the chair and talked away from her. Did you know Sally Groat was married?

Listen to me she said, look at me do you hear. I have got to get out of this place. Youre going to take me arent you? I must get out of here right away. Do you hear me darling?

He looked away from her. You will get out very soon he said, if you are quiet. What a nice view there is from your window. Do you hear me she cried, will you pay attention to what I say?

She would not speak to him. He was like the others. She turned her face to the wall.

Tell me what you would like he said, and I'll bring it to you. Have you everything you want?

Everything I want, Christopher how can you ask such a thing? I havent even a toothbrush. It was in your bag. I havent seen it, O I havent seen it.

What else do you want? I want to go home, thats all I want. Dear child you cant go home, not just yet. I am perfectly well. You have had a very serious breakdown he said. The hell I have she cried to him.

She told him what she needed. He took out a pencil and wrote it all down. Not the scissors and the nail file he reminded her. Why not? Its against the rules he said. But Chris I wont do anything with them. You had better not have them he told her gently. I hate you she screamed at him, youre in league with all the rest of them.

I want to kiss your hand, Christopher, why cant I kiss your hand? He looked at her and looked away to the snow. You must lie still he said, and let me do the talking. Will you let me talk a little? You have been very sick.

My baby Chris have I still got a baby? Where is he, cant I have him? Not yet, you can have him when you go home. I want my baby, why cant I have my baby? She turned again to the wall.

You mustnt ask, will you trust me? he said. No I will not trust you, you and Dr Brainerd and all the rest of them are trying to put something over on me, but I see through it all, she cried bitterly.

If you are quiet, he said desperately, and dont get excited and throw things out of the window. . . . All I threw was those nightgowns, they hurt my skin and I wont wear them. Why cant I have my own nightgowns? she pleaded. They cant let you have your own clothes he told her, for fear you will destroy them. Whoever heard of such a thing, I only threw those damn things out because they were so rough. Youre lying to me she cried to him. Christopher why do you lie like the others? She began to weep heavy tears.

Dont do that or I'll have to go he said to her. He got up and stood by her bed. He bent closely over her and walked away from the bed. Are you comfortable in that thing? he said.

No I hate it, my arms are bent back, Christopher why do I have to stay in it? Christopher she cried passionately to him, why have you gone back on me like this?

I havent Marthe he said to her. I havent gone back on you. I am trying to do what the doctors say. Youre not well yet.

I dont understand she said turning again to the wall, I thought you knew. Knew what? About me.

She told him. Now you see she said, now you can see how foolish it is for me to stay here any longer.

Its not true Marthe. Where did you get that idea? You must get rid of that. You must get rid of all these delusions before you can go home.

You dont know what youre talking about she shouted. You will see. And youll be left out. Only the ones who believe will be there. Even Mary and Mrs Welsh have sense enough to see that.

You mustnt believe what any of these patients tell you he said. Theyre all irrational and you must not believe them. Dear little girl he said to her.

She forced her head out of the hole in the canvas sheet. She stared fiercely into his eyes. Christopher! she cried. Her voice was like steel. Get out of here, do you hear me? Get out of here, and dont you ever come back.

He went out and shut the door behind him.

VII

They were standing in a line, each one with two nurses holding
her and wrapping her tight in strips of cloth. One nurse held the
figure still and the other sewed with large swoops, Marthe was
happy because it was the first time for her. Pauline had no teeth
and prattled in staccato German syllables.

I didnt know we were sewed for this. It keeps you quieter said
the nurse. It was Miss Sheehan. You ought to know better than
to act the way you do when youve had a college education she
said to Marthe. You ought to behave better than the rest.

The door opened and it was her turn. She marched stiffly
out, keeping close to the nurse. There was an orchestra of
laughter and strident sounds and down the stairs at the left
came a quartette of galloping nurses holding to the wrists of
someone in their midst who struggled and tried to bite their
hands. Marthe could not see the person in the midst for her
long flying hair. What was that? she said recoiling. Thats Mrs
Bodwell coming down again. Every time she gets let upstairs
she raises hell and has to come back down.

They went through beyond the stairs and there were the
tubs. One was empty and there were two faces in the others.
One face was red and sang frightfully, the other was quiet and
leaned to one side. Soft hair and an ugly smile on the pimpled
face. Who are they? Thats Mrs Higgins and thats Miss Weinschenck the schoolteacher. She turned away from them.

Here is Mrs Gail said Miss Sheehan to the gawky young
nurse who was on duty at the tubs. I cant shake hands said
Marthe. They lifted her into the tub. It was very long and she
lay in a sling. A canvas sheet was drawn over the top only her
head coming out. They put a small pillow behind her head.
Very slowly the water came in, tepid and smooth. It grew warm

deliciously. She glided her body about in the tub. She hung in space and tasted the green voluptuousness of living water.

The water kept coming in. It came from behind her and came around her and filled her body with warmth and listlessness. She was absolutely without strain, hung delicately in the water without effort or will. She was hung from the pivot of a golden sun and swung swinging in the pouring of its fluid content.

Now the tight cloth about her body became hot and irritating and she no longer felt the softness of the water. She twisted her body and turned her arms pinioned behind her, and rolled her body about. It was heavy and clogged the running of the stream. It was heat, languorous and clinging, and it pricked the pores of her skin. She twisted and fumbled with her fingers.

It was off, the spiral casket. She had reached with a finger, and torn the threads, torn them down the whole length of her body, in and out, and around and round, until the entire strip was unwound from her and kicked to oblivion below her feet.

Now it was essence of molten quicksilver and poured around her limbs and into her veins and swam about her lungs and went out at her feet. She turned her head to one side and the water melted into her eyes. The water was gurgling in behind her, constantly renewed, and out below at the bottom of the tub. Her arms long slender stems of pond lilies, and the water cress of her breasts floated and sank in the depth of the stream.

Its heavenly with that thing off she said. What thing? said the nurse who was sitting in a low chair behind her darning a stocking. The spiral wrapping. What do you mean? what have you done? Im out of it said Marthe.

You couldnt do it, how could you do it? Marthe fished below her feet with her hands and brought up the heavy wet cotton casing. She pushed a corner of it through the hole where her neck was. There she said, there it is.

The nurse was young and nervous. Put it back she said, or I'll catch it from the doctors. I dont see how you got out of it. How long can I stay here? said Marthe. You have got to stay until four o'clock. That will make six hours.

Who is that Miss Weinschenck, she looks so peaceful, why does she have to have these baths? If you think shes peaceful you ought to see her when shes out said the nurse. She'll kill you when youre not looking. The face in the next tub opened soft eyes and smiled like a crushed snake. Shes treacherous said the nurse, you want to look out for her. The head nodded and scarlet pimples stood out on its forehead. Then it turned away again and the eyes closed. She likes the baths said the nurse.

The woman in the farther tub, who had been sleeping for a short interval, awoke and began to sing again. Her voice was like metal instruments jarring together and there was a tearing apart of the edges. She sang from her broken teeth and her withered throat pulled out from the hole in the cloth and went up into her chin. She sang American jazz songs, and her head struck the rhythm for her voice.

If you dont let up on that said the nurse, I'll give you the towel. Shut up you goddamned fool said Mrs Higgins. She sang loudly and that which had made her screaming songs a melody was jerked aside by the ugliness of her intent. The nurse took a wet towel and pushed it into her mouth quietly, until there was no noise. The head of Mrs Higgins bounced about on the sheet and there were rich cursings from her silent mouth. There was imprecation in her livid cheeks and her forehead burned oaths into the warm and quiet room.

Cant anybody sing? said Marthe, does it bother the doctors if we sing? I dont care if you sing said the nurse, but I aint going to have any such commotion as that in here. The head in the other tub opened and looked at Marthe. Sing she said.

She knows I am God. She may be treacherous but she knows. Marthe relaxed her legs and arms and became a night blooming Cereus on the wrinkled stream. She had a small and tightly folded centre, yellow and full of gold and poppy-dreamings, and now she would open and pour out its fullness.

It came out staggering and climbed awkwardly up to the cruel height beyond it. They came holding sideways their golden bowls and climbed and climbed and found relief in sinking. They came each in their turn, stronger and more intent to stay. It was now a crying light and a chariot race to the far mirages in the sea, and up and up into the depths of the cream-incensed sarcophagus they whipped their fleeting runners.

It was a song, a perfect song, a note of clean and fixed control. It came to her in that moment, and in the drunkenness of sound she was in a trance of silver goblets and all her body became that song. She lay and was the instrument, and poured forth from her still throat a single needle-pointing cenotaph.

The face across the way opened again closed eyes. Sing again she said and looked with terrible intent upon Marthe. You can sing said the nurse, I dont mind that.

Ive had such a dreadful cold said Marthe, and I have had a hoarse voice for weeks. It just came back like that right now. Its good said the nurse, sing some more.

They had their lunch. Miss Ryerson sat on the side of the tub and fed them from a tray. Youre a stinking fool said Mrs Higgins as soon as the towel was taken from her mouth. She tried to bite the nurse's hand.

What time is it now? Its half past one said Miss Ryerson. The water was not so warm and she could not go to sleep. It had become tepid and stale. It slunk in murky hollows and she lay in a bed of soppy moss. I want to get out she said. You cant get out till four o'clock.

Marthe felt round the edges of the tub for the fastenings. Each one of them was securely fixed. She ducked her head down from the hole and left a dark space where her head had been.

My God alive cried the nurse leaping to her feet. Come right up out of there do you hear me, come out of there this minute.

From down under the sheet where her feet had been came fumbling Marthe's voice, muffled triumphant. I dont want to come out, its too cold up there.

Miss Ryerson thrust her hand down through the hole into the water. Take my hand do you hear she shouted down the hole. Take my hand, I'll help you out. Thank you said Marthe from the bottom of the tub, I like it better down here.

The nurse began frantically to untie the fastenings of the sheet. Marthe snorted in the water. Help help Im drowning she shouted. With fumbling fingers Miss Ryerson tore away the sheet and there she was propped on her naked wrists her whole head above the water her slim feet shooting about like the tail of a sunfish.

Come on, get out said the nurse, sighing deeply. You had the life scared out of me. Marthe stepped out on to the slippery tiles of the floor. Here get into this said the nurse and brought a warm bathrobe from the radiator. Get out into the next room. Marthe stood on the bathrobe and dried herself leniently with the towels.

Youre an awful one said the nurse, I dont believe you were drowning at all. I dont know what on earth Dr Brainerd will say to this, its the first time its ever happened.

I had to let her out Miss Ryerson was explaining. She got out of the wrapping God knows how and got down under the water. Dr Brainerd said, Dont you like the tub? You said you were crazy for it. She went in to see the other two women.

Dr Brainerd said Marthe, isnt there anything in this place that you can stop doing when youve had enough of it? Take care child, get into that bathrobe, youll get pneumonia. Dr Brainerd said Marthe earnestly, just because Ive got a toxic exhaustive psychosis is that any reason why I have to be treated like a dog?

Who told you you had a toxic exhaustive psychosis? said Dr Brainerd. You think I have anyway said Marthe, and some day youll be rather astonished when you find out what its all about. I dont think I'll lend your husband any more books said Dr Brainerd.

Do you want to see him? she said. You really want to see him? How can you ask me that cried Marthe feverishly from the bathrobe, when you will never let me see him?

Tomorrow he will be allowed to come. Now get back into your bed. I'll send a nurse in to take you back said the doctor. Well you didnt catch anything for that did you Ryerson? Maybe not said the nurse, but the next time you try anything like that it wont be so funny for you. Why what do you care if we drown? I dont said Ryerson, its just that Id lose my job.

VIII

A new patient had come and they had put her in the farthest corner. Mrs Kornfeld, with long skinny braids. She would not let them give her a bath. Pauline had got out of bed. Get back there Pauline. She doesnt understand English. Brunmark was distracted. I dont know any German she said, but I know how to make her get back. Leave her alone, I'll put her back.

Marthe had been quiet for several days. She had seen Christopher twice. You are ever so much better. He had held her in his arms. Why dont you kiss me harder? she said. He brought her a hair ribbon, blue of her eyes, and two books and some handkerchiefs. She hugged the books. I will read all the time. One of them was her green Shelley. She laid them away neatly and had not opened them. He brought some oranges and biscuits. She gave those all away. Chris my hair is so dreadful looking, straight and long. Your dimples dont show any more he said, you must drink lots of milk. They had not spoken of the other thing. Marthe had two pins which she had found and which she used to cut out pictures from a magazine. Christopher brought her a short pencil.

Why wont she take her bath? Mrs Kornfeld was standing naked thin and ugly. Her braids curled like snakes around her waist. Her mouth was sour and had cold sores around it. I dont want a bath she whimpered. Now you get up there and stop your noise. Brunmark pushed her over to the shower. She stood fidgeting and hunched herself under the water. Its cold she whined. Its not cold at all youre just too dirty to live said Brunmark. Marthe felt the water. Its not cold, let me give it to her. Why dont you want a bath Mrs Kornfeld dont you want to be clean?

No said Mrs Kornfeld. Here said Marthe and gave her the soap. She rubbed it gingerly on her knees. God Almighty said

Brunmark, I havent got the whole morning. Mrs Kornfeld shivered and dropped the soap. Let her go said Brunmark, I cant be bothered with her. She handed her a towel.

Pauline was next. She gurgled under the shower and her gums spread in smiles. She made rivers down her thighs with the soap. Mary Mahoney who never spoke and who had to be held under the water. She pinched the nurse. Thatll do for that, dont let me see you doing that again or the sheet for you. The skeleton came next.

Marthe had her bath. The shower was turned on with a key and came from a hose instead of from above. She was allowed to spray it on herself. She stayed in it too long and Mary stayed too long after her. They were the first ones out of bed in the morning.

There was dull noise out in the ward. Brunmark dropped the hose and ran to see. The new patient had pushed Pauline out of bed. You watch her will you, said Brunmark. There was someone choking in the bathroom. My God will you look at that shes trying to drown herself with the hose. What a life said Brunmark. She sighed strongly and took the hose away from the skeleton. For Gods sake Kornfeld arent you dry yet?

If you want something to do said Brunmark, you can clean the bathroom now while Im giving enemas. She turned on the water in the sink with one of the keys and filled a pail.

Marthe sloshed water about the floor and sprinkled soap from a box. She spread the whole bathroom with water and made trails of yellow soap powder. She was making a powder trail on a pirate ship. She took the broom and scrubbed it into every crevice. There were cockroaches and she scrubbed them into the floor. She remembered them from the very beginning, they were always in the bathroom. They were not in the hall or the bedrooms. She used to sit in the bathroom and charm them to make them go back. They knew she was God and always went back. Miss Sheehan said they could not be helped, that it was not because the bathroom was not clean.

It was free, it was a composition. The whole floor became the composition and she was making it. She pushed the cloth about with her feet, marching to and fro with swinging legs and watching the tiled floor go dry behind her. She would always clean like this when she got home. To make gleaming the hard surface, to make fine the edges and white the holes. She scrubbed the shower with the broom and after that the sink. She made glazed and prim toilets. She climbed to the window sill and smoothed it white.

Then she went back to the ward. Brunmark was struggling with the enemas. I dont need it this time Miss Brunmark, did Dr Brainerd say I had to have it today? Did you ever hear such a row about nothing growled Brunmark. God I'll never get through by noon.

The new patient had black frizzled hair and thick lips. Her face was freckled. She sat up in her bed with a pleased tolerant expression. Mrs Fearing wandered about in her gray bathrobe carrying bread crusts to the windows and pushing them out through the bars. Pauline was back in bed under her sheet waving her hands and singing. The skeleton was under her sheet her wretched arms flopping about muttering her chant.

Marthe sat down on the new patient's bed and began to write a letter to Dr Brainerd. She wrote several every day asking for things for herself and for the ward. Where did you get that pencil? said the new patient whose name was Luella. My husband said Marthe. You dont look old enough to be married. I am a mother said Marthe.

Whats the matter with you? said Luella. Theres nothing the matter with me said Marthe, I am being kept here for a reason. She went on writing the letter.

I was in a nigger cathouse said Luella. Marthe put down the pencil.

I saw stars and people's lives all going to hell. They said I was luney. Were you? said Marthe. No said Luella. Its much nicer here anyway. I know that Miss Sheehan. She was in charge of the Addison House of Correction.

Tell me said Marthe. Well said Luella, I dont know who my father was, my mother worked in the cathouse. I think my father was a nigger. She pointed to her hair. I dont remember nothing but doctors. Suddenly Marthe knew. Dr Armitage? I dont know the name. Yes that was the one said Marthe, you dont remember but I know.

I saw the whole Book of Judgment said Luella leaning forward. I saw the whole Book. Nobody would believe me. I know everything thats going to happen to everybody here. Yes said Marthe, but they dont believe you do they? Nope. Took six nurses to bring me in here. I was in the Strong Room for two weeks.

The Strong Room? Yes thats back of the tubs in there. They keep the ones they cant handle there. Only room for one at a time. Bed is fastened to the floor so you cant throw it. Every time they brought me some food I fired the whole damn tray at the wall. The dishes broke all over, she said excitedly. Broke every damn cup and plate in the place.

How did they feed you? Forcible feeding. Look at my arms. Got those from the nurses. What did you do to them? said Marthe. Nearly killed two of em, said Luella. O Im all right now, dont worry about me.

Mary Soulier had come to the other side of the bed and was sitting in a chair. She brought rags and divided them between the three of them. They sat quietly sorting the rags as Mary directed. The long ones for the post offices said Mary, and the middle ones here. Those are for the nuns. Shes crazy said Luella. The short ones, said Mary without taking any notice, are to go here. We'll save those for the men's ward.

Go on said Marthe to Luella.

She saw her coat through the door, her blue coat with the great gray collar and cuffs. Then it was there, they hadnt lied. Mary had come into her room with shattered eyes. I think youre going upstairs. Marthe leaned forward and clasped her hands. How do you know? I heard you were going today. I dont want you to go said Mary. I'll come back and see you every day. Marthe jumped out of bed and rushed out into the hall to get her clothes. Miss Ryerson was in the laundry and gave her the clean underwear and her stockings and blouse and skirt. Do you know if Im going upstairs? How should I know?

Youll get your own clothes upstairs, said Mary. Marthe was pulling on the heavy hard underwear, the property of the State of New York. It was rough and ribbed and yellow with cleanliness. She folded the long legs carefully as she used to do in the winter when she was in school and had to wear long underwear. A date in the spring and everybody in the school had to change on that day to summer underwear. She pulled up neatly the long heavy ribbed stockings and rolled them at the knee. She pulled on her own fleece-lined bedroom slippers.

The blouse was greenish white like the underwear and buttoned in the front. Then the skirt, round and tying in the back. It hung down to her ankles. She ran to Miss Ryerson who was coming in with a tray. Am I going upstairs? I dont know anything about it said Ryerson, but as long as youre here you can keep quiet.

Dr Brainerd came through the door and down the hall. She walked leisurely as if she were greeting friends between the acts of a play. Good morning Mrs Fearing how is your nose? The patients surrounded her and followed her in a supplicating group. Cant I go home today Dr Brainerd? Will you give this letter to my husband? My sister hasnt sent me my stockings.

Finally she came into Marthe's room. They all pester you so when you come in I thought Id stay here. That doesnt bother me, Im used to that. I am absolutely quiet said Marthe, dont you think I could go upstairs? We'll see said the doctor talking out of the window. Come to my office this afternoon. Have you been reading your books? No I havent had time.

Mrs Gails going to the doctor's. Mrs Gails going upstairs. Did you hear what Dr Brainerd said? Youll see Mrs Welsh again now, and youll eat in the dining room. She was going away from this, she would begin her life over again now and the first lap would be finished.

She sat in her room after dinner cutting pictures out of a catalogue with her long pin that she kept hidden under the pillow. Mary came in and began to talk about the puppies.

I really am going upstairs I think Mary said Marthe. I dont want you to go. Mary pinched her hand. I like you to stay. But

I'll come back and see you and anyway youll be going up soon yourself. No said Mary, I shall be here always.

You are not going to finish the song? Yes said Marthe, I know almost all of it now. She repeated the song that Mary had taught. Thats very good. You know the next part? I tell you now said Mary, and you write it down with your pencil. Marthe wrote it all down slowly and carefully. I'll know it all tomorrow she said, youll see. I wonder what time it is she said, putting away her pencil in her stocking. They looked out at the snow together.

The puppies are all dead began Mary again. And you are going away. She put her arms around Marthe. I cannot let you go. Her soft hair fell across Marthe's face. But you must go to your little baby.

Marthe came back from Dr Brainerd's office. What was it like? It was not anything, she reported. Dr Brainerd told her to sit at her desk and write her all the reasons why she wanted to go upstairs and she wrote seventeen pages and Dr Brainerd said that was enough. They had talked about death. You think a great deal about death dont you? I always have, but especially now when I am going to be responsible for it.

Dr Halloway had come in twice while she was there. She had on a navy blue cloth dress that fitted her closely and she had a red belt. Her hair was in regular waves. She wore tan silk stockings and brown leather pumps. She was young. But I am not going upstairs until tomorrow.

That night was a steel helmet set on a mushroom head. Godwin let her come out finally into the red hall and talk. At four o'clock she sent her back, but Marthe saw the lights go on in the early morning in the brick building across the evergreen tree.

IX

The sun came roistering down from high and slushed snow off
the roof of the East Wing. Little specks of sunlight shone red
on the snow. The birds flew around her tree in solemn cer-
emony and all the breadcrumbs glittered on the window sills.

She was going upstairs. She would wear her blue dress and
her Japanese dressing gown. She would have a brush and comb
and could rinse her mouth with glycothymoline. Nitroglycer-
ine, glycothymoline.

I'll have to hurry this morning Brunmark, I wont be able to
help you with the beds. Why not? Didnt you know I was going
upstairs? But you arent going till after lunch.

She went around bidding goodbye. I'll see you all again you
know. I can come back and visit whenever I want. None of them
ever do said Brunmark.

She went over to Pauline's bed and sang Die Wacht am
Rhein. Pauline drummed on the canvas sheet with her fists. She
thinks its the war. Marthe marched around the room singing in
staccato syllables. She led with a drum major's baton. Pauline
cheered and clapped. The skeleton stopped shouting and
stared. Luella got out of bed and followed Marthe around, her
nightgown streaming.

For Gods sake said Brunmark, get back to your room. Youll
never get upstairs if Dr Brainerd should walk in on that racket.

There was a strong stillness. Marthe sat down.

She had cleaned everything there was in the East Wing. She
had wiped the window sills and the bars of the beds. She had
done the bathroom twice and pushed the floor oiler up and
down the corridor forty times. Her room was starkly ordered.
She picked dirt out of the floor cracks with her pin and carried it
in a paper to the windows in the ward.

At last came the knock for trays. Marthe carried them around. She gobbled her stew and pudding out in the hall and went to feed Pauline.

Mrs Fenwick came in to relieve Brunmark after lunch. Goodbye Gail in case I dont see you again. But I'll come down and see you cried Marthe. Yes you will said Brunmark. She clanged out of the door.

Mrs Fenwick was large and had small brown eyes that squinted an Irish grin. My darling said Marthe throwing her arms around her, Im going upstairs. Never said Fenwick, who said so? Dr Brainerd. Im going this afternoon. Youre about well I guess said Mrs Fenwick. Take care now that you dont get into any mischief up there and get sent back again. Dont you worry said Marthe.

Listen Fat she said. Will I be able to go out on the porch and walk in the snow? I do wish you wouldnt call me that said Mrs Fenwick. I forgot, it doesnt mean that you *are* fat darling cant you see?

She was saying goodbye again to everyone. I'll be back every day to visit you all she said. Weve heard that before said Mrs Fearing. Luella and Mary were looking sadly at the picture books.

Marthe stared out of the window at the side of Pauline's bed. At the end of the brick building across the snow there was a fire escape. A nurse in a dark coat without a hat, her cap blown sideways by the wind, was going up. If she stops at the third floor and goes in I'll know. The nurse went up against the wind, up and past the second she mounted, on up to the third. She opened a door and went in.

A line of men came slowly out of the dormitory across the way and started down the walk. They carried brooms and shovels. They know Im going. She put her mouth to the window opening and began to sing. The notes were snow crystals in the upper atmosphere. The men stopped to listen and the men nurses hurried them on with dark surly commands.

Listen to me Gail youd better stop that right this minute if you expect to get upstairs. Everybodys quiet up there. There was a crunching in the big door at the other end of the hall. Mrs

Fenwick seized Marthe's arm and pushed her into a chair. Sit quiet and dont you open your mouth.

Down the corridor came the firm step of Dr Brainerd. Mrs Kemp followed her closely, begging to be let out. You are going to blister your feet Mrs Kemp if you dont sit down.

Marthe sat still in the chair, her shoulders back and her knees stiffly together. The doctor stopped in front of Marthe's chair. Do you think you can behave if I let you go upstairs? You really arent ready to go yet but Im going to see how it works. She went around to the other beds, stood talking a few moments with the nurse, and continued on out.

The door opened again to admit Mr Kornfeld. Hes such a nice man to have such a mean wife. Mrs Kornfeld lay in her corner bed, pulled up and sour. Her face was blotched and she sneered at her hair. Mr Kornfeld gave his wife a package of oranges and sat down by her. She seized the package and hid it under the bed. The minister came in to see Miss Stehli with his great round collar forcing up his chin. The collars too big the collars too big. You must come to the Sunday night service he said. The skeleton's sister came in with bundles and talked to the nurse, wiping her eyes and blowing her nose. She went over to the bed and spoke to her sister. The skeleton muttered her chant.

Then down the hall came walking a golden dream, redhaired and in a blue suit. His hands were outstretched. Marthe jumped high into the air and flung long arms about his head. Darling she cried, darling! I didnt know you were coming.

They went into her room, leaving the door ajar. You have to do that said Marthe. Marthe he said, youre so much better arent you? His eyes gleamed before her. You must be ever so quiet. But Chris, they think Im excited when I act perfectly natural. He shook out of his pockets oranges and chocolate and bananas. I saw Dr Brainerd coming in and she said youre going upstairs tonight.

Have you read the books? No I havent had time. Look. She showed him the pictures she had cut out with the pin. I use it for a nail file too. She gave him her pencil. He felt down in his pocket and brought out a knife which he opened and began neatly to sharpen her pencil. She was kissing his hands and his fingers. He looked at her as he pushed the knife.

The door swung wide and Mrs Kemp came in. Cant you do something for me mister? she said and took hold of Christopher's shoulder.

Now Kemp you get right out of here cried Marthe, this is my room and Im going to have my husband to myself for once. Cant you get me out of here? said Mrs Kemp. You look like such a gentleman Im sure youll do something for me.

Christopher dont you pay any attention to her, she talks to every man that comes in here. He looked at Mrs Kemp. I'll see what I can do he said. You will mister, you promise. Yes, he said. Mrs Kemp sat down on the bed. O what a miserable woman I am she moaned, and how lucky you are Mrs Gail to have your husband here.

Will you get out of here? said Marthe. Mrs Kemp said Christopher, getting up and taking her arm gently, I want to talk with my wife. O if my husband only knew I was here said Mrs Kemp, if my Tim—

She wont see him when he comes said Marthe. She wont have anything to do with him when he comes to see her. Do you hear what I say? she cried. If you dont get out of here this minute I am going to *put* you out.

I'll take care of her said Christopher. Mrs Kemp went over to the other side of his chair. You understand me mister dont you? You know what an unhappy woman I am, there isnt a woman here as unhappy as I am.

Marthe jumped out into the room and took her by the shoulders. Her face was a storming wind from the top of a mountain. She turned her round and gave her a push that knocked her out into the hall. She sprang out after her and took her falling hair in both hands and began to drag her down the hall. Christopher and Mrs Fenwick arrived both together.

You leave me alone cried Marthe. I'll teach her to walk in on me when Christopher comes to see me. I'll drag her over every inch of this floor till I get her in her own bed.

Mary Soulier came running. What are they doing to you? She leaped into the struggle and dug her nails into the nurse's

controlling bodies of other since she has so little control of her own

face. Christopher slipped and fell on the floor. He got up at once and got hold of Marthe's arms. Look out for that one he cried to Mrs Fenwick. Mrs Fearing was coming fast down the hall with blue cheeks.

Mrs Fenwick got her hands on Mary's wrists and twisted them thoroughly. O O shes hurting me. Marthe let drop the hair and turned swiftly in Christopher's arms wrenching herself away. How dare you hurt her how dare you Fenwick? She struck Mrs Fenwick with all her might on the side of her face and then Christopher pinioned her arms against the wall.

The room was tottering on yellow spindle legs. There were a thousand white nurses. You had better go Mr Gail. Christopher's white face with his glasses off. The throbbing of her wrists and her hair. I hope Kemp's hair throbs too it was all her fault. She turned her head wearily. Her hands were straight before her in canvas pockets. That for you you little devil Fenwick had said. Lets see you get out of that. Theyre having chicken in the dining room tonight said Ryerson. Too bad you cant have any. They were all angry with her, they said she had attacked them. She was under the sheet her hands were in pockets and the door was locked. The room was very dark because the sun had set. The sun had set over across the snow, floundered into a sea of iron, stewed in the red cauldrons of the gypsy's stealing.

From the other side of the door through the wall came piano chords and singing. She had thought long ago at the beginning that it was the Sunday nights at school when they sang hymns and each one chose a hymn. She chose hers for the music and knew all their numbers. Now she knew that it was the Gorestown State Hospital and those of the patients who were calm enough to participate were being allowed to sing. They were praying now, because the music had stopped.

God damn this world she prayed. God damn the people in it, the priests in red lace boxes and the lunatics in white wound sheets. God damn that piece of the sun that first swung away in lonely gas and trembled to cool itself to make a star. There is not a well of green stunk seaweed that does not bury its curse of sunlight and there are days of revelry in the bead-dripping basements of churches when rats run maudlin through chilled platters of song and the one-eyed draughtsmen mark grave arrows. God damn everything that cannot be made up into cheeses for Sunday lunches.

X

After lunch Ryerson came in looking for her. Mrs Gail? Come on get your things together. What for? Get your things I said.

Marthe reached under her pillow and took out her pencil, her pin, Mrs Welsh's prayer book, her green Shelley, a copy of Blake which Christopher had brought her, three handkerchiefs made from torn cloth, a sheaf of advertisements with jagged edges. Is that all you have wheres your nightgown? I threw it out of the window. You did? well youll catch it for that from Maude. You cant sleep naked this weather little fool. I cant stand that nightgown. Youre the only one ever complains about them. I dont give a damn I wont wear it. I want my own nightgown.

Shut up and come along Ryerson. She was glad when she could talk to Marthe. She was thin and sentimental, with strong legs. Whats the matter with you, has Charley turned you down? Ryerson squinted. I should say not. Well have you got everything now? Toothbrush? I gave it to Mary Soulier, she didnt have one. God on earth, dont you know better than to give away your toothbrush, whoever heard of such a thing?

The key was for her again. She and Ryerson walked out together. She was in the Day Room. She looked around it fast. Chairs, fireplace, the grating around it locked, table, ferns, magazines, faces. They went through to the left. Tubs? breathed Marthe. No, upstairs, said Ryerson.

They went up the long flight of stairs that Marthe had seen on her way to the tubes before and had never been to the top. She went up, each step on the feet of a newly born moth.

The great door at the top flung open to Ryerson's key, and clashed shut behind them. They were there. Nobody could take it away now.

Good morning Miss Wade. Heres Mrs Gail for your ward.
Miss Wade got up from her desk. She was a small blockhouse.
Her eyes were squint-lidded. She had a long smug upper lip and
her neck sucked in her chin. How do you do Mrs Gail she said,
as if she were at tea.

Marthe was looking about with straining eyes. There were
flowers. There were flowers in baskets and on plants. The beds
were in two rows, extending down, opposite, making a third
side at the end of the ward. There were people in some of the
beds, they were not strapped down. Some of the beds were
made up with straight white counterpanes. People sat by them
bent over without making a sound. There were one or two who
were mumbling silently. Miss Wade's desk was at the left of
the door at the head of the ward. There was a newspaper on
it. There were printed letters and a picture. She looked at the
paper. I wonder what the date is. There was still snow and it was
cold. That couldnt keep up for two years.

The two nurses took her down to the right of the door past
some private rooms. I dont want a room said Marthe, I want
to be in one of the beds. Well if you arent a funny one, said
Ryerson. Im sorry said Miss Wade, but Dr Brainerd has given
orders that you are to have a room.

The room had a bureau and there was a white counterpane
on the bed. She could see across the snow to the West Side.
There was a light in her room and a chair. Well goodbye said
Ryerson, mind you behave yourself. Wont I see you again? O
my God yes youll see me around. Have a good time with Charley
tonight. Ryerson came back a moment. Listen she said, this aint
a joke, hes asked me to marry him.

She came out of her room at once and saw that there were
other beds at that end of the ward too. It must be right above
East Hall here. She could hear a dull and continuous noise
underneath the floor. The same view only she could see more of
it. Great high windows looking out over the snow and the brick
buildings. A porch in front. I wonder if they ever go out on it.
Beds on the two sides and tables in the centre. At the side were
the windows and between them a couch. Chairs and people sitting in them.

Miss Wade took her arm and brought her over to where several people were sitting. Ladies, this is Mrs Gail. Mrs Glope, I want you to know Mrs Gail. She has just come up from East Hall.

How do you do said Mrs Glope with a gracious smile. She rose from her seat and took Marthe's hand. Her hair was done up on her head in gray snails and the ends looked out. She had large heavily washed blue eyes and sacks under them. Her nose was handsome and indolent. She was dressed in a variety of garments. She appeared to be between fifty and seventy.

Are you any relation to the Gails of Tuxedo Park? Cousins of mine said Mrs Glope. Do sit down and tell us how it is down in East Hall. Isnt it disgraceful the racket they make down there? Theyre really not at all refined you know, they are very ill bred. You must have been most uncomfortable there. They keep us awake up here sometimes you know. Very wild some of them are I fear.

I wonder if I am going to have my clothes said Marthe. My poor dear it is dreadful isnt it this State underwear. You know I have it on myself right this minute. I have so much trouble from rheumatism.

Who are these people? said Marthe. Come and I'll introduce you around said Mrs Glope rising. Do have some crackers. They passed around the crackers. Most of the people in the chairs gave no sign. Those who did, took three or four and ate them rapidly. Mrs Glope introduced Marthe to each one of them. They shook hands and turned away.

They walked down the corridor arm in arm approaching the desk and the long ward. They went over to a window. Here said Mrs Glope, beginning with a large sigh, we are in what is known as the Psychopathic Ward. We are what might be called the aristocrats of the place. Its the best ward in the institution you know my dear, the others are not so nice. You can see out here to the road, there goes an automobile. All the people who are well bred are in this ward.

But if youre not well bred? They have many other buildings said Mrs Glope, I really dont know anything about them. We have East Hall downstairs in this building and you know they are very vulgar down there. The better ones come up here from there but not many of them.

We need you here said Mrs Glope. Dr Brainerd was telling me about you. Dear Dr Brainerd she is an old and personal friend of mine. She told me you were coming and said I was to take special care of you.

Marthe was warmed. You are very kind. You see over there said Mrs Glope are the men's quarters. There are men here too? O yes my dear hundreds of them.

I dont believe she is a patient. But her clothes.

Are the people here all patients? Well yes said Mrs Glope, I suppose you might call them so. Of course I have only had a slight nervous collapse. Nervousness and rheumatism. Dr Brainerd is an old and personal friend of mine and always takes care of me.

They went over to Miss Wade's desk. Dear Miss Wade said Mrs Glope. *Do* you suppose I could have mayonnaise with my salad tonight? I really couldnt say said Miss Wade, youll have to wait and see. She was preparing something in a round bottle. Who is that for Miss Wade? Im going to paint Mrs Irwin's throat. Dear Miss Wade said Mrs Glope, she is always thinking of others.

Marthe looked at the lines of beds and she looked at the people in them. One of them stared at her but the rest paid no attention. They sat hunched up without moving. They really arent very interesting said Mrs Glope. They are so glum and they wont answer you. Its much nicer to have someone one can talk with.

A brilliant Jewess came out of one of the rooms and down to the desk. Her hair was worn down her back, soft and springing. She had a wide yellow ribbon about her head tied on top in a great bow. Her cheeks were scarlet bosoms. Her deep sprung eyes looked out from strong black brows. Who is that, who is that? I'll introduce you, said Mrs Glope. Her name was Annabel Neuman. She presented to Marthe a smile that streamed over white rocks. I have to sit and look at her said Marthe. They sat down together and Annabel was pleased.

Miss Wade who had been sitting sewing something and talking to one of the nurses who had come in now arose and put down

her work. She straightened her cap and pulled down her waist.
The dining room ladies she said from her chin. Excuse me said
Annabel, and got up. They began to pass out, some of them. No
Mrs Gail, you are not to go, you will have a tray up here. Marthe
watched enviously the straggling line. All of them hung back.

Come on Miss Wheeler dont you want your dinner? I
dont want to eat. Come on ladies, hurry. Miss Wade went and
rounded up the ones who had gone into corners. Come on
dont you want to go downstairs? I cant eat I cant digest my
food. Ive been here five years and I havent eaten so much as
a breadcrumb. Finally she got them all in the line and out the
door. You will have your tray Mrs Gail.

Marthe stood alone looking around the bare walls. She saw a
wide ribbon on a basket of flowers and went down the ward to
take it off. She wound it around her hair like Annabel's. She
touched a flower with the edge of her fingers. She licked the
petals and divided them with her tongue. She breathed in the
flower. There was a marking stick in the plant and she began to
dig with it. She dug up all the hard black earth around the plant.
She breathed excitedly. This was her garden again the one she
had had before the baby was born. She would make trim the
borders and round the bird pools.

What are you doing Mrs Gail, you mustnt touch those flowers. Where did you get that ribbon, you mustnt take things like
that. Miss Wade jerked the ribbon from her hair. That doesnt
belong to you. You had better go and sit in your room until
your tray comes.

I hate her and I will kill her some day.

Everyone had gone downstairs except the ones in the beds
and herself. There were two who were dressed who had not
gone down. One of them sat huddled up in a chair like a bird on
a bare branch of a tree. She did not speak. She had a face like a
thin baby bird. There were hairs around her mouth. The other
stood in a corner with her face to the wall. She had on a long
green sweater. She had a comb in the back of her hair. There
was a great quiet in the dormitory.

She sat in her room looking out across the snow to the West
Side. There were lights over there. Someone was coming into

her doorway. Here is your tray said Miss Baird. Im so glad
to see you up here my dear. She put the tray down. She was
tall and bountiful and her eyes were dim behind glasses. She
had gray hair that was streaked with brown. She had been a
schoolteacher in a small town. She was practical and liked
poetry. She had come into East Hall to iron sometimes and
Marthe had recited poems to her. Marthe remembered when
she was lying in the sheet and Miss Baird would come in and
rub her forehead. Why are you here Miss Baird? Im just a little
nervous and cant sleep. She lived on the West Side and slept out
on the porch. She said it rained in on her once and there was
sleet, she told Marthe how it felt. The porch is covered with
wire grating, you cant get out of it. I must go said Miss Baird,
I must get back to the dining room and get my supper. You will
come to see me again? Marthe begged.

There were two pieces of bread hastily smeared with butter.
There was a great glass of milk. This was besides the regular
supper. Marthe ate greedily. I have to gain twenty-five pounds
before I can go home.

The line leaned in again. They went back to their chairs. Mrs
Glope and Annabel came into Marthe's room. Such a meal said
Mrs Glope, no mayonnaise. Why cant I go downstairs and eat
with you? said Marthe. I dont know said Mrs Glope, it must be
the doctor's orders.

They say that Mrs Kemp downstairs is going to get put in the
Strong Room said Mrs Glope. She put up an awful row tonight.
We could hear her in the dining room. I thought she was going
to break down the door.

At nine o'clock the wheel chair was pushed in from the store-
room and they were to put their clothes into it to be locked up
for the night. You will have your own clothes tomorrow morning Mrs Gail. The thin forms stood by their beds in stagnant
attitudes.

Mrs Glope had lost her large hairpin and was wandering
about in search of it. She was in long underwear and corsets and
her black cotton stockings were coming down over her knees.
Her hair looked less abundant.

Very vulgar to have to undress in front of these people said

Mrs Glope. She went peering under the beds for her pin.

She doesnt have to come out if she doesnt want to said Annabel, she has her own room. Annabel stood up before the ward and took off all her clothes until she was naked. She had a sensuous soft body warm with life. She slipped her head into her nightgown.

Marthe took off her clothes too. She stood without embarrassment small and white. Your body is like a shoot of spring through muddy ground, said Annabel. Listen she said, will you pray with me tomorrow?

Then Annabel knew she was God. Mrs Welsh must have told her. She was happy. Where is Mrs Welsh? I havent seen her yet. She got transferred said Annabel. So Mrs Welsh was gone.

Why are you undressing out here? said Miss Wade, have you no decency at all standing there naked like that? Dont you know any better, go to your room immediately and take your clothes.

Marthe turned fiercely to Miss Wade. Why dont you leave me alone? she cried. Voices rustled and startled eyes rolled to stare upon her. Annabel ran to her bed. Marthe stood on tiptoe and stretched her arms and legs and made of herself a white shaft.

Mrs Gail will you take your clothes and go to your room at once? She reached out to grasp Marthe's arm.

She floated away from Miss Wade and down the long space in the centre of the ward that separated the rows of beds. She whirled in a black volcano and began to dance. The white faces in the beds drew back to the wall and watched her horrified, their eyes coiling.

There was a painted scarf hung from the mantelpiece at the end of the ward. She pulled it down and flung it about her body. She lifted up her limbs to the lights over her head and bowed down her body to her feet. She was a fair white stream gushing down the ill-poised canyons of a dream. She leaped into the gyrating space of night star falling. Down she fell into an abyss of crowded murmurs and up she swept again to peaks of light. She was a comet in her dream a shooting star loosed from the portals of the rainbow's chilling. She fled and fled away down the long labyrinths of her childhood's darkness and into mazes of fine winding through which she spun and wheeled and crouched to die. . . .

Doctor shes wild. She belongs downstairs, said Miss Wade. Her chin was rattling against her teeth. She'll stir my patients all up.

They were muttering among themselves and shaking their heads. They were nervously twitching their bed clothes and murmuring that it should not have been allowed. They mumbled their lips together and chafed their hands. There was a low rising and falling of their voices like a wind on a roof. Dr Brainerd said, you dance beautifully, you had better put your nightgown on and go to bed.

XI

In the morning Miss Wade was pleasant. Here are your clothes
Mrs Gail. She lifted a blue bundle out of the wheel chair.

There were her clothes. There was her blue dress with the
finely pleated skirt. There were her shoes, her tennis shoes. Her
own shoes with rubber soles and heels. No more no more no
more. She kissed them. She folded the hospital garments in a
round bundle. O to throw them far out the big window, far out
into the snow, beyond the walk beyond the trees beyond the
sun. No she must give them back quietly, soberly. She must
never by glint of eye or ear betray those guardians of her demol-
ished past.

Youll have to wear that underwear said Mrs Glope unless you
have heavy underwear of your own. But why do I have to? Youll
get pneumonia this building isnt well heated said Mrs Glope.
Yes said Miss Wade, you must wear the underwear.

She was dressed now. But where is my belt? and I havent any
garters. You cant have belts here said Miss Wade. They strangle
themselves with belts.

I'll ask Christopher for pink garters with green flowers on
them. You see explained Mrs Glope, the rest of us wear corsets
and dont need garters.

Marthe was sliding down the summit of the morning. She
had on her blue dress, dress of jersey blue, tailored and neatly
trim. She strutted up and down before her mirror. No more no
more of the green white skirt that hung from her tight waist and
dropped on her legs. This was short and very free and she could
kick the light from it. It had a soft round collar of tan silk edged
with scarlet. The cuffs were tan and were scarlet edged. I love it.
I love this dress. The belt had been red and she wanted the belt.
She looked earnestly in the glass. If my face were different, it

looks so funny. It was white like flour and her eyes were coming out of it.

I love these shoes. They were old and one of the tips was off one of the laces. They were tan and large and had soft rubber soles. Her stockings were tan silk. Silk stockings, long and cool. She had rolled up the drawers above her knees and her legs were long and round and silk-encased.

After breakfast Miss Baird brought her the rest of her clothes. Dr Brainerd had given them to her to bring up to Marthe. Put them in your room and take care of them. Marthe stood alone in her room and spread her things out on the bed. There it was, her great soft voluptuous Japanese dressing gown. There were folds and folds of it. Unfold the yellow dragons and the green and yellow storks. She put her face in it. It was free. She rebelled against the dressing gown, the wide flopping sleeves, the softness of its folds. She laid it away in her drawer.

A small pink nightgown was in the towel. It was long and had no sleeves and flowed down her body. She would have the sweetness of that nightgown now forever. She put it on the dressing gown and shut the drawer. Her sheepskin bedroom slippers warm and old.

The white brush and comb, a new green toothbrush, tube of paste. There were cold cream and vanishing cream in new tubes. Christopher had done this. Glazed round tubes beautiful and smooth, white and red virginity. Handkerchiefs writing paper and envelopes. She laid them all away.

In the afternoon she was by the window when a lady came in to see one of the patients. She carried a baby in her arms. Marthe ran over to her and gazed at the baby's mouth and sputtering eyes. She seized upon his fat hand stuck out, and he turned his head and looked at her. His hair was yellow and went up to a point. Let me have him he is mine!

The mother drew quickly away, backing to the wall and holding the baby close. She reached out with her hand, her eyes were round with fear. Miss Wade came swiftly and said, Dont be afraid. She told Marthe to go to her room. Marthe went passionately to her room. She crashed the door with all her might and stood alone. This earth is made of tar and every morsel is stuck upon it to wither. The snow was outside and there were orange peelings lying in the snow.

She got up early before there was a sound in the ward, to see what might go on. She went on her toes to the bathroom to see if there was anybody there but there was only Mrs Glope's hair-pin and some lost towels. The nurse lay sleeping fat and red at the desk with her white cap sailing in the little wind that blew from the open windows. All the snores came from the long beds and out of one room behind the desk a small cry that it was prison and could not get out. Marthe went comfortably in her flowing bathrobe with great yellow storks, fishes rent with blue, to a radiator that was near the window and out she stared upon the snow. There was one person in the bed nearby, the other beds were white and flat. Marthe Gail looked out through the bars upon the blue glassy snow, ridged with the diamonds of the early sun. She could not see the evergreen trees that stood below to the right, that had been from her window a green pyramid of sparrows. Across the snow, across the closely meshed footprints of those who could walk in the snow, there was the sun, coming like an Oriental bride across the treetops and the cold brick walls of the outbuildings, coming with black braids and cobwebs sucked from the fire walls of the night.

Marthe stood before the window at the far end of the ward, opposite her room. The nurse could not see her, the desk was at the other end of the corridor. It had come to her now that there was to be no release, that this would go on for every morning and that most of the mornings would be gray-risen.

The radiator made bursting sounds of water being forced from below. The beds stood around flat and clean, with neatly turned counterpanes for the occupants who were not there, and small furry wads of dust around the castors where the brooms and carpet sweepers had been turned back. In one of the beds lay a woman with gray braids, snoring with an orange in her fist. The little pieces of sunlight began to form in their accustomed places on the floor and far out across the outbuildings she could hear, by pressing her ear in the crack of the window, a rooster crowing. The rooster crowed and he was standing tall and stern on the top of a wire fence, clutching with carefully bent ridged claws on the wire and screaming his beak to the early sun. And the sun was coming and the rooster would fly with awkward spread wings down from his perch and begin to peck the manure heaps.

At about this time there was stirring in the room next to Marthe's, and out of the thrust door came Mrs Glope her hair high with pins and papers, enveloped in towels and nightgowns. Her nose squinted away from the light and her mouth shaped itself to pronounce the cold. With stiff fingers she pressed boxes of soap and powder toothbrushes salves and bottles. Good morning Mrs Gail she observed with champing teeth, how can you stand there in that draught? She went on down the hall to the bathroom and stopped to pick up the things that dropped as she went.

My baby had the cleanest and smallest finger nails I ever saw, they were like flakes of onion skin.

Crackers and oranges came up for her after breakfast. Christopher had sent them for her. She wanted his warm hands and his over-hanging shoulders. The great mountain shoulders that had been the Wall of China when she wanted his face in the night.

She took the box of crackers and went down to the long ward at the other end. Mrs Glope walked with her, fondly linking her arm. My son is the greatest ornithologist in the State of New York, I'll show you a picture of him if youll come to my room. Marthe walked so fast that Mrs Glope was left gaping.

By the bed stood one of them, with black gray braids drawn over the top of her head and bulging eyes. Her jaw was yellow and wrinkled like a horse's. I cant digest a thing she said looking greedily at the crackers. She says she cant eat a thing, she says she hasnt any bowels. No bowels, I havent digested a morsel of food for five years. Go away from me do you hear. She wore a spotted calico dress and carefully picked threads from it, rolled them up and put them in her mouth. Go away do you hear, she muttered without looking at Marthe.

A woman with starting blue eyes came out of her corner and went past Marthe, making a turn and back again to her bed. As she passed Marthe she muttered sideways, You are a damn fool and ought to be let out of here.

Look shes eating your crackers. Bowels is eating my crackers, I thought you said you couldnt eat. Couldnt eat she couldnt eat. I wont digest this I havent digested anything for five years. She was sitting on the edge of her bed winding her hair. The flowers were hers. I think you can have the ribbon. She looked at Marthe frightened. Marthe wound it trembling around her head like a bridal coronet. Like a coronet of stars wept out of the mist. Bowels had cow eyes and a soft mouth. She spoke perfectly, very slowly. The magazine was hers. O please let me read it. Its got words in it and I havent seen any for so long.

Now you give that back to her, commands from the desk. You are not going to take people's things away from them like that. But she doesnt want it. That doesnt matter, you go and sit in that chair.

She sat in the chair and her body became a hot iron to brand Miss Wade with ashes. She was a furnace and Miss Wade would be burned in her, howling and helpless, arms and legs. Her legs would curl up like dying newspapers, crisp and billowing. I will burn her, I will burn her heart.

She sat eating her crackers, munching. Then she began to cast them at the beds. Some of the patients caught them, some drew back protesting, curling their hands. She hit Bowels accurately on the top braid of her hair. Help help, squeals of help. Feeble and swallowed, smothered and down. The desk looked up from the sewing. Whats the matter Miss Hurd? She hit me with crackers, whimpered far. I did not, shes lying.

You had better go to your room Mrs Gail and stay there. She marched out, her ribbon bobbing, her posterior indicating the desk. Annabel laughed quietly.

She didnt stay in her room. She shifted out by careful planning, and was in the front ward by the windows without being seen by the desk. There flowed into a great chair Mrs Flynn. She showed Marthe all her medals. You must pray for me darlin Im bloated. She taught Marthe prayers for each medal.

I wonder if its true after all and she knows it. You must pray for me darlin, your prayers make a difference. Mrs Flynn ate all the crackers. Eat every one of them. Im bloated and Ive been here seven years. They talked about Mrs Glope. She gets handy about taking things and they send her here said Mrs Flynn.

You are to go downstairs after lunch said Miss Baird. She brought the tray and took Mrs Flynn back downstairs. I sit here for company said Mrs Flynn, I live on the West Side.

They are almost done on the West Side. I cant go there ever.

I wonder why youre to go downstairs said Mrs Glope. Marthe had found a pussy willow in one of the flower pots. She had looked at the flower pots and there had been the pussy willow. Mrs Glope walked away disappointed.

Then it must be that it was spring. She touched lightly her fingers to its edges and pulled it across her lips. Softness of spring tight to the lips. She stood in the middle of the floor and heard no words. Then suddenly Miss Frink (Hazel who had fed her with milk) unlocked and unopened the door on to the porch and swept dust balls out over the snow. Spring, spring, spring with sunstream and pussy willows and snow in the sun.

Marthe darted behind the nurse and out to the snow. She scuffed her feet in the snow and plunged her hands into its stiffness. She sat down in the snow and laid her head on its gentleness, on its decorous propriety. Get up this very minute and back into that room. The pussy willow. It isnt spring at all, where did you get that idea, its winter and youll get pneumonia.

She came downstairs carefully and carried the pussy willow. You must be very quiet said Miss Harrison, to show that you are better. O hello Brunmark my darling how are you? Brunmark had a pail in each hand her face was set. What are you mad about now Brunmark?

They were walking across the Day Room to and from the wings. The faces were there of the ones who were not walking. Marthe stalked by them. Here you are said Miss Harrison and opened a door. There were the hollow eyes, the stone well eyes, that had wheeled her into East Hall. Black stars in a white night. Sit down there said Mrs Wendy, do you know what is going to happen to you? No. You are going to have a marcelle wave. Your husband has arranged for it.

Then it was true. She was going to be made over now, her body even as her mind was new. She sat down and looked at her face in the glass. What room is this? Dont you remember, you had a catheterization in this room? It was white and had a long table covered with a long white pad.

Her face was so thin that the hair seemed to be a part of it. Her hair hung down from the sides of her face in long swoops. Her face was white as the room and the hair hung wearily.

When it was done she looked in the glass and there were rings of hair around her ears and across the top of her went ridged waves neat and circular. I am beautiful.

My God where did you get the curls? Brunmark coming out again with the pails. She was going into East Hall. Want to come in and visit? No no. Not today. I thought so said Brunmark.

The pussy willow had bright living in it. When they came into the dormitory upstairs everyone stared at her hair. Mrs Glope came fondling with her fingers, running them through the back. Be careful not to get it wet when you wash your face. Miss Wade smiled cheeks and chin. Very nice she said, see if you cant behave now that you look decent.

XII

Now it was all true and there would never again be doubt. She was God she was God. If it could not be known by the singing this at least was proof. She could write again. Again as in the lanes and among the periwinkles with her father she had wandered to the cowbells' marching, when she had built towns and settlements in her forehead with a long branched stick and had invented the names for all, now this was again and it could be put down. She had all the paper and Mrs Fearing gave her some more. It would all be written down and the thousands of pages would be her witness. She had said it all, now it was all to be written, and this would be the proof as had been the Lion and the Bull.

The fever came upon her to write and the fever was her distress. If she could sit still to write that would make it come, but instead she refused pills with her feet strung against up the wall as she had done in nightmares at school when they had found her screaming, and leaped in her bed when the mattress was being aired and led the orchestras she had so long understood. These things prevailed, the singing and the orchestra. Down to the left where piped the flicking flute, heels clicked and up to the drums. And above all she must have a swimming pool for sliding with facile shoulder to the island beyond. The dancing she could not give enough to, and in her wide-sleeved storks she made decorous the gestures of the walls.

I could walk in the water they could show me the water and it would be very easy. The dream is the only thing and in a dance across the pond I would make a crevice for their sighs. She sharpened the pencils, and across the white frailty of the scrap paper went the black strong torrent of her dream.

It had been in the hay with a box of chocolate almonds, in the rain, and a sudden leap from the high cave into the hay. Down into its smell and depth she plunged, down to the settled straw beneath it. And always on the ladder on the other side her father whistled the Mill Song and the Sextette. He would have to go back to the city to push an assured pen across to the end to the period and back again to the period after the M. It was he, he contained within that rigid fence. But this was he, this more than ever her father, munching apples from the tree and saying come away dont look when the bull was in the pen. That was the part she did not understand and this was the part he gave her to understand.

That night she cried aloud in her sleep and the nurse was afraid. You will wake them all up, there will be a scene. The nurse moved her bed out of her room and down the hall to the desk. Marthe looked from her bed down the ward where they all lay hunched under their shoulders. One of them sat bolt upright and slept.

She reached for her sheepskin slipper and rocked it in her hands. He is sleeping in it and I will rock him. Papa les petits bateaux qui vont sur l'eau, ont-ils des jambes?

You will have to stop singing, it keeps them awake. But you idiot this is my baby and he has to go to sleep. There was rustling and eyes popped from bed to bed.

I cant sleep Miss Wright. I dont know what Im going to do with you she said, I'll have to have you taken downstairs to East Hall if you make any more noise.

Someone called the nurse at the far end and she went down the hall past the rooms. Marthe slipped from the covers and went over to Miss Lanier's bed and sat on it. Miss Lanier's long eyes shook. You mustnt stay here she shivered. Go away go away said a voice across the aisle, modulated in the throat. Marthe went down to where Bowels was sleeping quietly and blew in her ear. You can have some more crackers tomorrow if you want them.

The woman turned suddenly and screamed into the ceiling. All the beds began to tremble and all the voices began intermingling, stooping and rising. After the scream there was only the movement of the voices, like the waters of a lake when a wind had passed.

Miss Wright came fast from the other end and Marthe was back in her bed. All the voices indicated Marthe, all the hands pointed terror fingers shaking at her bed. All the heads were shaken grimly and some of them rubbed their hands across their woollen nightgowns and some began to braid their hair.

Miss Wright rang a bell and stood looking at Marthe. Presently the keys came from the other side and it was Miss Sheehan in white and black-browed, sweet to the touch and gentle.

I cant keep Mrs Gail here, she is keeping everybody awake.

Whats the matter Mrs Gail youve been so quiet lately? Miss Sheehan stood looking too. I cant sleep and she wont even let me sing.

Perhaps youd better come down in East Hall, just for the night. O no no no no I will be very quiet. Dr Brainerds off said Miss Sheehan to Miss Wright, and I couldnt get an order. If she makes any more noise send her down to me. Now Mrs Gail said Miss Sheehan, Irish and smooth and down in her shoes she likes noise.

She turned her face to the wall and closed her eyes. Soon there were circles on the wall, pointed like the ones Annabel had made for her valentines. Mrs Fearing was coming upstairs they said, and they would make valentines. Come come come come, valentines for the doctor's wife. Annabel was sleeping there in that room right across there to the right. They had given her a room and she was sleeping in it. Miss Wright may I go in to see Annabel? Will you go to sleep? cried the nurse.

She was in a blanket in a chair by the desk. That if you wont move. She sat up there and watched the ward go back into slumber. Some of them saw her and began to fret again, chafing their hands. There was the heaviness of sleep in the night and the nurse nodded at the desk and went into circles. The blanket was too heavy and had been warmed at the radiator. It would make a large ponderous dance to be danced in mud and under dripping eaves.

There were eaves in this room and she could make them drip. She would practise the dance. All the drag of the blanket went into her lagging feet and into her ears went the music. The beds stirred again and drew back against the wall.

Its no use Mrs Gail, get your slippers and come with me.

She began to cry O no I will be good, O please dont take me down down down that stairway. Just for tonight she said. O no no no I cannot ever go back there, O I will be so quiet.

They went down the stairs together. If you will behave theyll let you come back up said Miss Wright, so dont make a row. The heavy blanket trailed up behind her, up into the quiet places.

Now Mrs Gail. Miss Sheehan shook her head with pursed lips. You that was being so good. She unlocked the door into East Hall and Marthe was delivered.

Into the red light and the black warmth of the hallway went Marthe, back to the strange sounds of the dead bodies under the sheets. She blinked her eyes and saw Miss Godwin. My sweet Godwin let me sit up and talk to you. Whatve you been up to, I heard you was going home soon. Voices down the hall. Pauline praying for the Kaiser. Sarah Kemp marching. Other voices, new voices one young and high yelping a puppy.

Up and past them came Mrs Kemp heavily trodding and with strong intent. How do you do Mrs Kemp do you remember me? You poor woman aint you out of here yet cant you do anything for me? said Mrs Kemp. Same old line said Godwin. Old bitch said Mrs Kemp. Thats me said Godwin.

Marthe went down to her bed and got in obediently to go to sleep. It was a bed in the ward in the midst of the voices. O my brother my sister my God my God.

She did not sleep and the noises grew in volume and increased in weight until her ears shouted to each other, and round and round in the circles of Annabel went the lullaby she had sung in the sheepskin slipper. She sang it stridently. There was an instant of absolute silence, even the skeleton, then with triple confusion came forth loud words from every mouth that heard. Gradually the curses fell away until only the skeleton was left droning my brother my sister my God my God.

Marthe came out of a dream. Someone was walking up and down in front of her bed. She blinked the red darkness and it was Mrs Kemp. She was pacing and rubbing her hands together. O my God my God will I never get out of this. Marthe got up and followed her to the other end of the hall. Mrs Kemp turned and looked at her. Ive had enough of you, she said. She struck Marthe in the face.

All then Marthe was a yellow disc flame merging from blue into satin, and hung and hung her arms to stare. She forced out with her long and permanent hands and beat into that tiger dream a halo of resistance. She struck until the rays of the sun had gone oblique and there was only a loosened drop of blood on her little finger and her face had become a nesting place for swallows. She went calmly to her bed and slept.

It was something she had seen before. It was longer than she had seen it before. The head, the smile, the smile, the long and knowing smile, the pimples that stood out above the smile. The snakelike sliding of the eyes to tempered sounds, to sounds that she herself had made of music softly moulded. The tub, and water sliding warm.

I want to sleep with you. The voice was arrowlike and brought no response. Stone arrows made by treacherous warriors of the Tibetan plains. And stood out from her face a leer of indigo.

How did you get in here? said Marthe calmly. She knew, she recalled swiftly all that Ryerson had said. She is going to kill me and has come quietly to do it in revenge for the singing.

I was in that bed and I woke up. It was the harsh arrow voice of a child, an elderly child that has sharpened the edge on the varnish of a kettledrum.

If you will go back to your bed I will sing to you, not the way I sang in the ward but the way I sang in the tub.

I want to sleep with you, sing to me here. She put a hand in her nightgown. Marthe knew that she was reaching for the knife and that if she screamed it would be after her throat was slit from spine to spinal column.

She remained in the bed. Dont take your hand out of your bosom she said, because if you do I will never sing to you again the way I sang in the tub.

Blotches were on the white face in the moon. I dont want your singing I want you. She took her hand out of her nightgown and began to unfasten the button at Marthe's neck. There was no knife there was no knife. Now she would reach down her throat now she would take from Marthe her blood and suck it into a slimy pipe to be delivered elsewhere. I must not stop it now, I must not make a sound, it is my baby, this is for me because my baby is dead and I could not give him sustenance.

I am going to scream and then I shall be dead, I cannot keep down a scream. She could not move her feet, all her body was an iron spear, set to the floor and could not make a movement. Her hands could not reach to keep this thing away, she stood and stood and not a breath stirred from her.

I am screaming I am screaming from my bowels and from my neck and feet. I scream and scream and there is not a little wind. Her back began to give, and in the corner between her ribs and her hips on the left side there bleated and froze that frightened spot that always when she was waking from a nightmare trembled through her.

Feet coming fast and keys and in was Godwin panting red and white. Whats the matter?

She sank upon the bed and said no words and quietly back to the other bed went the schoolteacher on her toes because the floor was cold.

XIII

What am I to do with you? said Dr Brainerd in the morning.
Please, the West Side? No said Dr Brainerd, you cant go on the
West Side. Will you try me upstairs once more?

To Mary and Luella she spoke and they talked together at
the window, leaning to the snow. When I am out you are coming to live with me. Mrs Fearing would not speak to her and
stayed alone in her door-barred room. She is going upstairs said
Mary, and doesnt want to have anything to do with us. Pauline
went by for the baths, and Luella. Pauline kissed her hands.

Mrs Kemp sat muttering in a chair and turned her eyes
whenever Marthe passed. I dont know what you did to her said
Brunmark, but whatever it was thank God for it. Im afraid I hurt
her, I know she hurt me.

Did I hurt you Mrs Kemp? No word and not a look. Im sorry
if I hurt you she said. She leaned over the chair troubled and
stiff. Yes you did you little bitch, and turned her head away.

Well said Miss Wake, I hear you got sent downstairs last
night. She smiled without showing her teeth and her lips folded
over each other. Yes I did. She walked past, back to her room.
The people downstairs are more interesting, she informed Miss
Wade in getting past. Why dont you stay down there then, you
cant imagine how quiet it has been here without you.

It was the school again and that was Miss Fillmore the music
teacher who sat at the head of her table and scorned her. Her
teeth were too small from the measles and she smiled from
yards of pink gum. Her nose glasses dropped from her well
shaped nose and she gave them glove menders for Christmas
after she had said I have sent to New York and they had
expected large dolls with French hair. And when she came back
from the weekend where she had plunged white toes into the

tide, and sat again at the execution, Miss Fillmore said How quiet it was with you away, and had sent her from the table for crying in the milk.

So she would kill Miss Wade, kill her in remembrance of those shining gums that said, How these children have twined themselves around my heart, and would not let her sing the solos when her father came. She remembered when her father had walked with her along the dusty road, shoes gray with the dust, she with her long branched stick and he listening to her. I didnt know he said, why didnt you tell me? I hate her I hate Miss Fillmore, she is cruel and she has been cruel all these years, and she is thin and mean and I will kill Miss Wade.

And then it came, just at that very time, the letter, the first letter from her father. It was his writing, blue ink and straight slanting to the end, large going and rigid. She opened with a pin and read it, all the words, down to the very end. The end, the very end. She took it and showed it to Mrs Flynn. To Annabel she showed it and when Mrs Fearing came up and spoke to her she showed the letter's end.

Then came the next morning Miss Sheehan to take her downstairs. You are going in the tub today she said, and Dr Brainerd said that you were to eat in the dining room.

She stood on the mat and let them sew her up. Sheehan you are mean, you are pinching me. I think she knows. She is pious and she pinches me to get revenge.

The water came warmly around her. It would be for six hours. It was not for punishment.

Miss Sheehan was mopping up the floor of the tub room with her skirts pinned up and rubbers on her feet. You must keep on behaving well she said, and not have any more setbacks.

Miss Sheehan do you believe in God? Why do you ask me that? If you had enough faith you would take off your glasses. Miss Sheehan sloshed around the floor in the soap and stream. Im no Christian Scientist. It doesnt matter, you believe in the second coming of Jesus Christ dont you? Yes said Miss Sheehan. She turned on the water in the sink and filled the pail again. You didnt know it was going to happen in your time did you? It might happen tomorrow said Miss Sheehan. Had you ever thought that it might not be in the form of a man? What then? It might be in the form of a woman.

Miss Sheehan turned away. Youd better not talk so much, she said. She went out taking the pails and the broom.

Brunmark fed her the lunch from a tray and told her about her new love. Brunmark had met a great many crises. William Brunmark is my husband. Bill Brunmark is *my* husband. They had decided to wait until he came home. When he saw them both together there in the kitchen he sat down suddenly and said My God. Then he said a little later, The best thing to do is to flip a coin. That was enough for me said Brunmark, I lit out and left them together.

Her hair was warm in waves. Brunmark had admired it every time. It was twenty minutes to four and the cloth weighed upon her body. She must not get out, if she stayed to the end she would be free. My hair, all neatly waved. It came over her as she sank into the cloth that this could be the proof, if she wet her hair to get to Christopher then they would know. The bitter thing to do, I will wet it for Christopher cried she in her ears, and quickly ducked her head. All wet and slipping to the neck her hair clung fine.

What are you up to for Gods sake cried Brunmark suddenly turning. How did you get down? My neck said Marthe, I know how to bend it. Your hair you fool said Brunmark look what youve done. I did it for Christopher, now it is wet I have no beauty and all I want is him. My God said Brunmark, you are the very limit. The limit I am, and the end of it, and you do not know what end.

Brunmark told her she could get out before it was time. The cloth was heavy but she had done it. The sheet was unfastened, and down began to sink the water, down below the grave straps and down to her wet and sagging body. Down sank the water, down and down, cold and heavy and still she was left in the empty tub. She was in the ground, rolled down on the straps, a wet and sunken corpse, bound close in the cerements of the grave and lying chilled and paralyzed beneath the ground.

Come on out of it. Brunmark pushed her shoulders and propped her back until she stood up, wound, a mummy of the sea. With adept finger Brunmark found the thread and ripped and tore and snatched the windings, unwound and unwrapped until she stood alone and wet a little cold upon the floor. Here out here, and she pushed to the other room towels and bathrobe on the radiator.

This was the proof of all, now was the time come, she was quiet and controlled, her hair was wet, and the water had rolled away from her.

XIV

The day was Sunday. Now for the first time she was to see the dining room, and eat her weight in gold. You have got to eat enough to gain twenty-three pounds the doctor said, and then you can go home.

Mrs Fearing took her arm and they went downstairs. They sat in the Day Room, ferns drooping green, and faces on the wall. They sat and waited for the bell. All the faces leaned drearily to the ground. Dont they want to eat? said Marthe. No said Mrs Fearing, they have lived their day. She sat in one of the chairs and Mrs Fearing talked to her. In the dining room she said, nobody makes any noise. They eat with forks and dip their bread. Down the hall from the West Side came white hair smiling like a queen. Who is that, who is that? Thats Miss MacDougal. She plays the piano. She stopped by Marthe's chair. I am so glad to see you my dear your face is so refined. Marthe rose and took her hand. I hope you will be with us a long time she said to Marthe. She spoke clean direct cutting English, perfectly shaped the vowels. Her hair was cream of white, and hard distinguished nose and chin. She carries herself like an Infanta of Spain. Miss MacDougal walked from the room. She washes her hair in urine Mrs Fearing said.

Now who should come in but Mrs Welsh, fat and chirruped out of her chin. Marthe rushed to her. Where have you been, where were you all this time? Sit down said Mrs Welsh, be careful. I was in 33, Im eating here today. What do they do in 33? They stand about and dance, some of them iron their hands. But why were you sent there? Hush said Mrs Welsh, a nurse will send you back. Then suddenly the bell swift and short, electric in its speed. They walked quietly out and through the corridor.

It was not as large as she had imagined. A dozen tables, round, and people coming in and sitting down. You are to sit here. There were two women from upstairs but they did not speak. They looked aside and began to eat their bread. She stared around the room and there was Mrs Glope. My dear Mrs Gail, said Mrs Glope, nodding her balls of hair, how good to see you here. I shall send you some of my mayonnaise. She was surrounded with bottles and little plates. A chicken carcass was on one of the plates and she put mayonnaise on it and a wisp of lettuce. She touched the top with mustard. She called to a nurse who was standing by. Take this to Mrs Gail she said and nodded.

In the middle of the table was an enormous pitcher of milk. There was a bowl containing sugar. The large thick plates were piled at one side and all the knives and forks were in separate piles. This is your napkin said a nurse, will you do the serving? She plunged the large spoon into the wheeling stew and dished out evenly the meat and white potatoes. Give that to her said someone, I dont like gravy. A youngish girl said thank you. The air was heavy with no one speaking. She passed the forks and the knives. Her joy melted down to gravy and silence. The knives were short and blunt pointed and the forks were gray.

Will you have more stew? I do not know your name. No she said, and turned away her head. I never eat. She offered to each one. They shook their heads, they munched their bread. There was one from upstairs who had black hair drawn into a small ball at the back, torn back from her ears. She chafed her hands. How are you feeling today? Marthe asked of her. She turned her back and looked into her gown. The young girl on her right spoke softly to herself. She moved her lips delicately and cut her stew. Its a good stew said Marthe politely. She moved her lips ahead.

Marthe looked across and saw Mrs Glope eating thick her specially reserved dishes. She hovered over plates and bottles like a summer cloud, shading them. Her arms went out like the wings of a pelican to cut her meat, her napkin was raised to sop her chin. I wonder if she is going to eat everything in all of those bottles. Those are her own things suddenly said a voice, she sends out for them and pays for them. Marthe looked to see who spoke but all the faces were still.

The dining room was peaceful, a gentle purring sound punctured by a sharp laugh. The nurses stood in the corner by the sideboard and talked among themselves. What is it to them or God above that we eat and sleep and dream? The nurses waited for the last one to drink her cup of warm tea. There was no sound now, only the muttering of the nurses. The other tables waited menacing. Marthe folded her napkin and sat expectant.

Now said Mrs Mills, and the tables flowed sluggishly together. The people formed a sullen line. You are to stay to help, and you and you. Those were detained by Mrs Mills. She was a small and very pretty little hen. She propelled ahead of her the three, reluctant. They protested and shook their heads. They dragged their feet. I want to help, I want to slosh suds upon bright pans. The line moved out and Marthe went with the line.

Down the hallway past the ferns and into the Day Room. Some of them remained there and sat in chairs and some went through and up. Marthe came into the Day Room and saw a fire in the fireplace. She ran to it, she stood and warmed into it. There was a large fine black grating about it, padlocked at one side. She sat, and in the fire lickings a quiet came to her that had not come before.

The logs snapped, and darted glints of fire into the room, and fell back from the grating. Viciously the flames leaped up the chimney. The logs settled underneath like piles in the undertow. Great scorching strength came from the fire and she leaned her face to it and her cheeks grew scarlet burned. No one spoke to her and there was no one there she knew. The fire was her peace, she was of it and alone and still. It snapped and bit and hacked the tender kindling.

A loud harsh metal clanging and a clack of heels gone fast dripping down the corridor. Into the room and before the fire spread Letty mountain breasted and her legs like veals hung up for market. With sudden jerk her great backside she plunged upon the floor. Thats a good fire screamed upon the listlessness of warmth and sunken clay.

Marthe turned to Letty and her eyes burned deep within. Go away from me or I will spear your flesh. Letty's smile was above her dumpled chin, and under that the drop of flesh right-angled to her neck. Her great gobby breasts shook with each redoubled laugh and she patted her bosom to check her gurgling. Ohohohoho—she went into a snorted whisper and shook her ears to her hair. She wore golden ear-rings hung with pearls and shook them into her hair.

When did you get here? she finally cried. Tonight said Marthe, and I am going to take an iron to brand your heart. Letty snorted again and trembled on the floor. I been talking to Dr Halloway.

O how is she? said Marthe quickly. The straight body and the golden feet. Ive got all her laundry to do tomorrow said Letty. Just got it from her, all silk she wears and little pink shirts. What do they look like? Nothing touches Dr Halloway but silk I know because I wash em. What do they look like? Different colours said Letty patting her breasts, lavender and pink and green. All matches, pants and shirts and stockings, all chiffon. Marthe looked into the fire where spun chiffon stockings on a limb of ice and hung into the icy sky to dry. Doesnt she get cold here in the winter without heavy underwear? The snow, the frozen snow. Not her said Letty, shes got a fireplace in her room. And it has no grating, it has no grating.

Letty's voice upstarted to the doors. Why dont you play the piano? she said. Can you play the piano?

Marthe got sudden to her feet and ran from the fire to the piano standing near the ferns. She laid her hands upon the keys with deliberate coldness. She touched with one stiff hand four notes she had known before, then went softly into their strength.

They came like fluttering phantoms out of dimly lighted corridors, and all at once she plunged with two hands into the keys and came swiftly from beneath her hands the portion of the dream she had been keeping. Gold and black and even, the full crescendo of the dream, up the keys and into the black beyond. She leaned her body to the keys and bent her head above them and from the wide spaces between her fingers burst forth yellow birds to the sun.

Youll have to stop playing the piano because we are going to have the Sunday service said Miss Baird. Marthe turned to her from black eyes shot with fury and remembered not to speak. She speared one foot into the polished surface of the under side and left a small and finely rounded mark of white. What have you done? O look what you have done. Im sorry, Im sorry, Marthe shouted to her trembling glasses. Miss Baird regarded with worried eye the mark. You are very quick to anger she said, you had better take care.

Too quick Miss Baird, tomorrow I will take oil and leave no sign.

They brought in chairs from the dining room, putting them in rows one behind the other and across. You must be absolutely quiet said Miss Baird. Yes I know she answered peevishly, the Lord God wants no noise. You must not speak that way said Miss Baird, you know you must not. Marthe looked at her with terrible intent. You are but my people she said softly, you cannot know what is in my soul.

They went up the stairs and told Miss Wade. Ladies the evening service. The line was shorter than for meals and no one was urged to go.

Down the stairs they wandered, shawls about their shoulders, hunched into their chests. Annabel wore a bright green ribbon on her head. Mary with long soft hair and heavy clothes to her feet. Marthe took her arm. Mary's eyes were no longer lit, they had died. She was quiet and serene, her mouth drooped above her body. I must know her again, this is not her warmth.

They took their seats slowly, each one where she came to. There was no clamour, the seats were gently taken. Marthe held closely the limp arm of Mary. She looked at her and saw her spirit's defeat. Mary's face drooped white against the red cushion of the sofa where they were, it was very still and made no sound. An alabaster disc.

Into the room came Miss MacDougal smiling her skirts into position. She sat down on the piano stool without abruptness and putting her sharp glasses went thumbing through the sheets of music. A rustle in the midst and Marthe turned. The door in the back had opened. In came a tall red priest, his collar choking his chin. A small and dumpy woman came, and Dr Brainerd. Marthe looked at Dr Brainerd as if her tongue were loosed. Dr Brainerd looked back at her and lifted her hand. Her eyes were worn, and slumbered.

Good people he said lifting up his chin, and his blue eyes popped. Let us sing Hymn Number 176. She turned very fast and it was Now the Day Is Over. The piano went gracefully into the gentle chords and played all through the hymn. Now he said, and they rose and went into the song.

It came to her again as before and she sang all through it with the burning flesh in her eyes. She was standing in a little room and there was a piano playing in it and all of them were standing about, all of them singing it. And she would save their end. They would die and be crushed into a coffin and she would raise them from death and from carousing life. Especially would she save them from life, bitter in its fulfillment. And love and death and life, not one of these things for good.

When they had finished he made a sign for them to sit down and they fell into their seats. Marthe looked for Dr Brainerd but she had gone. Some of them knelt before their chairs and some bowed their heads into their hands. There were some who made no sign and some were laughing to themselves. She looked from her eyebrows to see.

Dear Lord we are gathered here tonight to give Thee thanks for all our blessings. Some of us are almost done and some Thou hast scourged and given more than we can bear. The fire is going out in the other room and there is no one there to see it. All the masses of quiet and relief. The hands before the face. But we do not complain to Thee Our Father we ask Thee for greater strength. Ah yes for greater strength. Not for Thee O not for Thee but for ourselves. We are here and made to parade our lust, and of that dying tree above the snow is our flesh made. We ask Thee for greater strength to bear our cross and for our loved ones to bear theirs. My loved Christopher, and my father's face. I am here and they are there and before their judgments will be mine. I will judge them of things they know not of. I will go to prepare a place for them. We ask it in the name of our Lord and Saviour Jesus Christ. And that is I.

The priest opened his eyes in relief and shouted another hymn. Miss MacDougal spread into the tune and they stood up to sing it. Get up get up sang out the nurse in whisper from the back. Bowels stood up suddenly with a hymnbook held loosely in her hand. Mary came up out of the ground like a lily and swayed beside her holding to her arm. Marthe held the book before her eyes and did not look herself. That I should know these hymns, that I should know them. I am the resurrection and the life. I am the poem of the earth, that contains all manna and all release.

They sat down again and he stood awkwardly before them. He spoke to them a little and groped for words to say them. Annabel changed softly her place and leaned to whisper, Hes going to tell us a Bible story she said, and sat back primly. She was laughing in her soundless mouth. Marthe could see her laughing.

He spoke brightly. She put herself where he stood and saw the crooked lines. The nurse was like the rest, not desiring. Miss Baird looked intelligently at him and nodded now and then. I must look at him now, no one but Miss Baird is paying the least attention yet he goes warmly on. She looked with comprehending eyes and lips that foresaw and soon he was talking only to her. No less this night to him than Sundays in his presbytery. His hair is harsh and falls in the back on his collar in which he is ridiculous. I have told him so but he laughs because it is a bughouse. He does his duty like an early soldier.

My good friends. His wife has seven children and I am here. The pains of fifty women could not make his face shine less. Annabel said into her ear, I think hes a converted Jew, thats why hes so intense. He thinks I am listening to him, he is poor and very noble. He longs like us for peace and there is his flat hat.

And now my friends we shall sing Hymn Number 321. The books began to rattle and the faces came into significance. They sang it to the end and he bowed his head. May the Lord watch between me and thee . . . while we are absent . . . one from another. He turned eagerly to Marthe. What is your name I have seen you before. My name she said and looked him in the eyes, is Jesus Christ, and you cannot bear that to your purpose.

He turned away, embarrassed. Do they pay you anything for this? she asked him. Of course not he said eagerly, I go to the Penitentiary too.

They went upstairs. The hot milk came up on a tray, the milk that had warmed her the first night she had spent abovestairs. She went to her room directly across and talked back and forth with Mary as she undressed. Mrs Hopeman hugged her orange and snored into the wall. Marthe opened her door after the nurse had closed it and listened for the night sounds of the ward.

Below the floor someone was pounding. The wind came down upon the snow and swept it into spirals that were cold before the windows. The wind whirled the house about and up into the air it dropped and fell upon the snow, and scattered with it all the oranges held in all the snoring hands.

XV

In the room there in East Hall, the room that Marthe had had
for so many months, she was lying, turned over and her broken
teeth sighing. Mrs Trowbridge was in charge and no one could
go in. Then when the other nurses came and the doctor from
the other side the door was left ajar and Marthe looked in
through the crack. It made her sick to watch it and she leaned
away from the door and looked again.

In the late afternoon when the trees were growing into deserted stalks of winter she began to groan, not as others had
groaned but wearily. She groaned and expanded her lungs and
out again it came. She lay on her back and there was no movement only the sound of her lungs. She is going to die they said.
I know that sound said Mrs Welsh.

Marthe stood at the end of the ward beside the window and
looked upon the dark room where she had lain in pain. She was
here in this place, she had come to visit, and there was to be a
death. She stayed to watch the death. It was the other room she
saw, it was in her mind, the room of the hospital, where after
the sword had gone into her and she had expelled its edge she
lay quietly, holding the pain. I am about to die, and Christopher
has caught the death. Round in circles went the baby, in the
white circle on the wall where she had thrown the medicine
glass. The breast pump had hidden her face, when Posy pumped
it came out round and when Christopher pumped it was faint
and clear. I do not want to die, I love so many things. I love the
things of life, there is not any solace for this death. Cold hands
laid soberly across a pallid breast, hair soft to the touch, eyes
unclosed. They stare, they stare ahead. Christopher lay quietly
on the side of the bed, if he lies there she will be quiet and I will
close her eyes. He closed my eyes and sat dreaming before

them. She looked and looked again, and in her room was a creature creeping, around the floor, around the bed, up to the bed.

I must get out of this she cried and moved from the window. She went quietly to the nurse. Is the woman in my room dead? Yes said the nurse, Mrs Higgins is dead.

She lies there on my bed and does not breathe a groan. It has gone out from her and all the injections of a summer's afternoon cannot bring back to that bed her flimsy hands. Its gone now and there is left the injected body. They will soon lay a sheet across the face and a mass will be said in other places.

Later in the evening two men came in white suits and followed them into the room the nurses. Out came all of it at once a stretcher bearing, white and stiff she lay beneath the enfolding sheet. All of the eyes were watching, all of the lips said what they thought.

Now she is gone said Marthe, she was the one who sang gutturally in the tub and they would not let her sing. She screamed obscenely and no one heard her. I think she had syphilis said Mrs Welsh, but can you die of that? They die of that, they die of that, they die of many things.

Now in the corridors she was being carried, out to an ambulance stood in the snow, down to the undertaking room. There they would see her, whoever they were, her friends and children and grandchildren. There he would break up, break into crackling ice and putting his hands before his mouth. There he would stand alone with her, with no one to cool his head and rest his feet. She would lie smooth and unwrinkled her mouth set in a crumpled smile and the redness gone from her face. The teeth would not show and the hands that dug long nails into the wall would be freshly folded on the breast. Only the half would show and all the mourners would pass and sign and look and go away, shuffling their feet to the music. And he would wait and with flooded brain would lean and touch a hand to the forehead and in the other breath would go direct to a chair, set apart and remained folded. Death and the dancing of sun-worms.

The next morning Mrs Trowbridge in the bathroom. My God said Brunmark, I thought I would have died when he came in. I was closing up her eyes and I says to Stark for Gods sake get a window weight to keep these peepers down. And in he come said Brunmark, black and his handkerchief. And right after him Dr Armitage, if you can imagine that. I know said Trowbridge, Stark and I nearly dropped her twice.

Shes dead shes dead shes carried off and all the walls make merry. Shes dead like my baby and her hands are crisp.

XVI

Before you go on the West Side you have to go to Conference.
She had heard of that. Once a month the Board came and those
who were ready to go home were taken singly before them and
the doctors. It was very solemn. You generally have to go twice
before you get out said Mrs Welsh.

They were sitting upstairs in the back ward and Mrs Flynn
was rolling out of her chair. Marthe had helped Hazel do all the
cleaning of the ward. She had rubbed down Miss Wade's desk
and received a filtered smile. Dr Brainerd came by when she was
watering the flowers. You are getting better and you will see
your husband today. Miss Ryerson had brought in the janitor
and he had jerked the radiators. Thats Charley, that is her
Charley. Mrs Fearing started making valentines. She was quiet
and spoke nothing, she wouldnt come in Marthe's room but
watched for her.

You are to go for a shower after lunch. Coming out of the
dining room with all the gravestones nodding she met Mrs
Fenwick. Fenwick I am going to have a shower in the shower
room.

It was Brunmark who came to take her. Get undressed here
and put on this bathrobe. They went through the Day Room
and turned to the left in the short corridor instead of passing
through to the West Side. Through the room where they had
curled her hair and into the shower rooms.

Now quick in there. Vaguely she remembered. In that tub
that long warm tub her rings had slipped off. Where are my
rings Brunmark? Come on come on, get into the shower. White
and shaking she darted into the compartment and Brunmark
stood before her at a distance to play the buttons and turn the
spigots. From all four sides came fine prickings, warm and

comely. The needle spray. Marthe danced lifting her legs and leaning to the spray. Brunmark bent to the turning of her bright nickel spigots, leaned to hold the hose that rushed at Marthe's spinal column, played it up and down the middle of her back, holding her out and erect like a stone majesty. Brunmark's cap fell to one side and she shifted her feet to the changing of the waters. Dance dance Brunmark, throw away your cap and dance. Come out from under your stiff legs and float above the spray. Be still be still Brunmark cried out above the rush of the spray. They laughed and shouted and the water mounted and leaped and fell again.

This one is the last, watch out, she cried, and suddenly from below sprang up a rigid strand of water. It took her off her feet and up into the air she went and snatched above her head and hung, glorious in the glittering and spuming all about. She hung from the pipes above her head and turned and twisted her long swinging legs and all her body about. She swung her legs above her head until she hung as in a tree above looking down on green water and yellow foam.

Then quickly all the spigots were shut off and on again straight and stiff did Brunmark set her cap. Get down from there do you hear? I wont get down I shall stay up here forever and you nor no one else shall ever bring me down. She curled her legs about the pipes and hung her arms below.

Of course you know that if you dont come down youll have to go back to East Hall. Brunmark went composed into the other room and laid the edges of her cap before the glass.

So down she came, quickly humbly like an ape that has been too long in treetops and sorrowfully seeks his food. She put on her clothes again and looked at her face in the glass. Do you think I am getting to look not so drowned? If you would behave yourself you would be out of here.

But no one cared and in the marsh there was singing of the frogs. It was winter here but not aloof from the frost, and the white chipped box of Mrs Higgins had gone down. That for her, perhaps the snow would cool her head, the white grave clothes for her father to resent. He had stood above her bed and she had cried to him. Long he had stayed and laboured in her love. He had come up in the pullman train and had wondered what it was. She his dream gone springing into the canyons and he climbing slowly down for her and wetting his feet in the sluggish river. Her father's light high up on a peak of solid rock, and rattlesnakes that he had killed for her treasures. Perhaps again he would come, whistling in the lather of the early day and kissing her head above the morning. When the gas light had gone off he was standing there laughing and saying that she was to make the biscuits again, round and gold and dropped into the pan. And his retching sobs came from the other side of the closed door and she shook her feet and went out from where he was.

It must not be forgotten, she told him in the fast dying leaves that spun by on the sizzling road, when fast into the sunset they swung the throttle and vanished, that you have been the one who saw and you have been denied. I will make a vow she said, and it shall be for you.

There was trouble with Mrs Glope. Mrs Glope took her tooth-paste, her slippers and her towel. Where are my things? she cried and looked and looked. She would find them with Mrs Glope. Why do you take my things? I dont take them my dear, you left them in here. The nurses said she must watch her property. If you cannot take care of your things you should be in East Hall, they said. Mrs Glope came in sideways mincing and asked to see the pictures. Will you please go out? I want to think. My dear said Mrs Glope, it is all the same whatever we do. I want to tell you about my son.

Her son was the greatest ornithologist in the State of New York. He owned part of the county, the largest part. Mrs Glope prayed for him loudly. She would sit in a large chair at the head of the ward in the evening when they were all undressing for bed and she would pray for different members of it, and for Miss Wade. Miss Wade was a Catholic and asked Mrs Glope not to pray Protestant prayers. But my dear Miss Wade here we all are and we're all the children of God. I would rather you didnt pray at all said Annabel. I would not pray for you said

Mrs Glope, you are a Jewess. Yes said Annabel, shaking her thick hair and brushing it away from her forehead, thank God for that. You crucified the Lord said Mrs Glope. It was fun said Annabel.

Marthe put her head in Annabel's lap and she brushed her hair. Go to bed said Miss Wade, you cannot stay up any later than this, they are all in bed. She could not find her nightgown, the soft and silk. It was not under her pillow. If that woman has taken it I will shout her shame. She went into Mrs Glope's room and spoke to her. Madam, have you stolen my bridal nightgown? I did not steal it said Mrs Glope, you left it in here. This is too much, I will take her ornithologist.

The next day she went into Mrs Glope's room and took three bottles of salts, cream for the throat and hairpins. She took the large sepia photograph of her son. She put them under her mattress.

At half past one came Mrs Glope sidling down the hall in anxiety. Her hair was unpinned and her hands were dry. I cannot find my cream she said to Miss Wade. Marthe watched her and said I will help you search.

They searched up and down the hall, and in Marthe's room. I think you took them said Mrs Glope, in return for the nightgown. Miss Wade I think Mrs Gail has got my salts. You will have to take better care of your things said Miss Wade sniffing at the newspaper.

The whole day and part of the next Mrs Glope went about softened. I wouldnt mind the salts she said, but they have got my son. She searched and she talked. Where is my son she cried to all that came in. Miss Wade put down her foot. If you cant take care of your things you will have to go back to East Hall she said. O were you in East Hall Mrs Glope? cried Marthe, I didnt know you were. I was not said Mrs Glope, Miss Wade, I was not.

Marthe put all that she had taken back again when Mrs Glope was out. What? there they all are, I knew someone took them. She walked to Miss Wade with the picture. Here it is she said, someone has taken it. I told you. Who is that? said Miss Wade. It is my son she said.

I took your picture you silly old fool because you pray so much. I took the salts because you stole my nightgown. The hairpins you will need again. From this time Mrs Glope looked suspiciously upon her and did not any more come in to touch her hair.

Annabel came running to her room. Theres going to be Conference today she said, and you are going. How do you know? I heard the nurses talking theyre coming today, and you and Mrs Welsh and Mrs Fearing.

I'll tell you how to act, be sure not to let them catch you in anything, be cleverer than they are. What will they ask? Theyll try to catch you up in things to show that you dont know whats going on. Remember to be quicker than they are, it wont be hard she said.

It was true, there was the Conference that day because Mrs Fearing was sent for first. Be good said Marthe to her, and leave your nose alone. Mrs Fearing looked back with dignity and settled her small blue apron.

They sat around at the far end of the ward. Mrs Glope was sorting envelopes and cards and was occupying the whole table, the little slant-legged wooden table that folded up at night. I wish you would go away from me said Marthe, I am trying to read and your talk is incessant. You are vulgar said Mrs Glope, you came from East Hall. Well why dont you pray for me then? said Marthe.

Mrs Glope let fall the cards and spread her fingers wide. She lifted up her head and threw it back against her neck with closed eyes and mouth in prayer. Dear Lord she prayed, her deep voice pitched in trembling supplication. It shook her body and her head shook with her voice. The others stared and one or two of them closed up their eyes. Dear Lord she prayed, I pray Thee to watch over this my sister here beside me who has been led astray from Thy paths. She has come up here into a group of refined persons from a wicked and adulterous generation down below.

They are not adulterous, they dont get the chance to be.

Mrs Glope opened her eyes and closed them up again. Dear Lord she prayed, help us to make pure this Thy servant who has been in evil ways, Thou knowest that down below us here Thy servants are not as other men are. They speak vulgarly and fight with their hands.

Dear Lord said Marthe, Thou rememberest well that this Thy servant Glope was also downstairs, and Thou rememberest . . .

I dont know what you mean, who told you such a thing?

. . . That she once so far forgot herself as to slap one of the nurses who insisted upon pushing her into a bathtub which she desired not . . .

Open your eyes, you ought to be ashamed of yourself, how dare you say such things, who told you that? Mrs Glope came swiftly from behind her table and snatched at Marthe's hair.

. . . Dear Lord Thou knowest how Thy servant Glope hateth to take a bath. Make clean Thy servant Glope and finally in Thy good time (and make it soon) lead her into Thine everlasting kingdom.

Let go of my hair this minute or I'll give you the pounding of your life. Mrs Glope let go and drew back. She drew back and shouted like a round ringed hornet's nest that suddenly had been broken into. Her words went wild and circled round and stung uselessly wherever they lighted.

Whats all this? Miss Wade from the other end. You go to your room Mrs Gail. You had better be careful how you behave today.

Is Mrs Gail down there? Down the hall came fast Miss Macauley who had charge of the Day Room and the West Side. Miss Macauley white and spring and trimmed at the waist her pretty legs going briskly by. Come with me she said when she saw Marthe. She took her arm and marched her down the hall.

The door shut behind them and shut out Miss Wade and Mrs Glope. Conference, Conference. You saved the day, I was just going to tell Miss Wade where to go. O you mustnt do that, Miss Macauley spouted a giggle.

They went through the Day Room, out to the left past the piano and the ferns, through the dining room to corridors beyond. Marthe staring madly saw a great room full of pots and a streak of people washing dishes. The kitchen said Miss Macauley, its almost time for dinner. They went on down the long hall and at the end was a small door. Pushed open and there sat a grave gathering of people. Dr Armitage at the desk like a schoolteacher. Mrs Fearing sitting stiffly in a chair near him before all the people. As they passed through to a room at the back Marthe saw Dr Brainerd turn to look at her.

In the next room was a mannikin in bed and the head of a man in plaster, indicating the brain centres. There were other mannikins, and a skeleton and charts.

From the other room came Dr Armitage's regulated voice. Will you bring Mrs Gail in, Miss Macauley? Her stomach was hurdling and there were vacancies within. Mrs Fearing walked slowly out and Dr Armitage indicated the chair at his right. Miss Macauley deserted, let go of her hand and slipped into a seat at the back. How do you do Dr Armitage? said Marthe.

I must be absolutely composed. He rose politely and indicated the chair. Marthe sat down and crossed her legs and looked about the room. She could see far in the back Dr Brainerd with a smile about to break. Dr Halloway next to her, intent. Marthe noted her sport sweater. You have too many goodlooking clothes she said to her across the room. A titter blew through the back row.

I wonder what this is. She noted the doctor who had given her the spinal injection and there was the minister who had been there on Sunday. How did you get in? she asked him across the faces in between them. They all began to laugh. Dr Armitage rapped on the desk. He set his face and began.

Now he said will you tell us your name? Why you know my name said Marthe, you said it just a moment ago. You will have to be serious said Dr Armitage. I must warn you that this is a serious business. I advise you to answer every question I put to you, simply and truthfully.

Now do you know why you are here? said Dr Armitage putting his head on one side and looking at her like a parrot. All of the doctors were looking at her, and one was pulling his beard.

Im here because I think Im Jesus Christ.

The entire room exploded in a great shout in which Dr Armitage was caught before the others. They laughed and shook their sides and their faces became wet and they leaned to each other and laughed. Dr Brainerd shook her head and took off her glasses to wipe them. Dr Halloway brought her head out of her lap and Miss Macauley settled her cap.

Dr Armitage sat up and rapped the desk. He pulled out his watch. Now tell me Mrs Gail, do you remember coming here? The room sat expectant, all their faces alight and on the edge of breaking out.

I remember coming here. I called everyone a damn fool as I recall it, I believe I called you a damn fool Dr Brainerd . . . I believe I was rather violent. I understand I—

Thats enough said Dr Armitage. Do you know what brought on this, ah, state?

Why someone told me I had a baby. Of course I dont know, I havent *seen* the baby. You dont seem to be very strong here on having our relatives around.

No said Dr Armitage. Now tell me where you are.

Here? Yes.

Dr Armitage! Dr Brainerd, I appeal to you! You over there in the corner with the long-winded prayers—do you all really think I am so crazy that I dont know where I *am?*

Well if you know tell us said Dr Armitage.

My dear doctors, I am sure that as alienists you have no superiors. But surely when its written all over the sheets, and the blankets, *and* the laundry bags, not to mention the letters I receive from home, you cannot believe that I dont know this is the Gorestown State Hospital of Gorestown. I may be insane but I protest Im not feeble-minded.

You can go said Dr Armitage. (I shall be gone.)

If in departing I may be allowed to mention she said, that such violently checkered socks do not go well with such a dazzlingly striped tie (being an alienist of reputation you must think of these things) I am sure you will not take offense. Perhaps we should speak to Mrs Armitage.

There isnt any Mrs Armitage called out Dr Brainerd from the chorus.

Marthe rose from her chair. Dr Armitage got up and bent over her hand. Goodbye Mrs Gail he said, I hope I shall have the pleasure of seeing you soon again. She shook his hand and held it for a moment. My dear Dr Armitage she said, when I have risen from the dead and have restored my kingdom upon earth, if I can do anything for you or yours a word from you will be considered of the utmost importance. He does not know my heart.

Miss Macauley snatched her arm and rushed her out.

XVII

It was the afternoon and she was sitting with Christopher on the sofa in the hallway that went over to the West Side. Here is a package for you he said. She tore away the strings. There fell to the floor a small pair of round garters, silk palest blue and edged with a flimsy rim of yellow fragile lace. Joyfully she slid them over her shoes and up above her knees. Look they have pink flowers and tiny yellow stamens.

He turned away from her face. I cannot see your white skin. Swiftly she leaned to him. O my darling she cried to him, I want your body, I have dreamed it in the night.

Christopher got up quickly. He put his hands to his face. There must not be any of this, I will go. No no she cried to him, and stayed his arm. No darling I will not kiss even your hand.

He sat down, a little away from her. He brought out of his pocket another package. She took it from his hands. It was a small white paper bound book, heavy with uncut leaves. When did you get this? she cried. She held it delicately between her fingers.

I am going to cut the leaves for you he said, bringing out his knife. She gazed out the window upon the snow. I am well Christopher she said, I am going home.

Plenty of time for that he said and slit the first page violently. I am going home she said. They sat in the shadow of the dark afternoon. She put suddenly her face against his cheek. I must have you she cried, it is all a dream, I am not Jesus Christ. I must have you to hold tightly my breasts, and you will kiss them to your death.

He got up quickly and walked to the window. They were passing through to the West Side with trays. Miss MacDougal nodding her tower of hair, Miss Baird erect with self-conscious

smile tripping her feet and balancing her tray. The others passed,
Miss Vaughan with shining trumpet hair turning her head away
with pursed lips and eyebrows that scalded her forehead.

I want to go home, she said. There isnt anything the matter
with me now, is there?

Its slow he said at last, looking back to her from the window
and the snow. Its very slow. You must trust me he said. You
know how I want you. He turned his eyes back upon the snow.
Dont come near me he said sharply, or I will go away. She
bowed her head and sat upon the couch.

Listen Marthe, he said to her. He sat down beside her again
on the red sofa. I have something else for you. He reached into
the inside pocket of his vest. He gave her an envelope. I almost
forgot he said.

She took the envelope from his hands and looked within.
There was no letter. She looked again and put her fingers down
and pulled out a spear of tightly bound hairs. Its his hair said
Christopher, I cut them for you.

She held the hairs in her hand and stared upon them, yellow
and soft. He took the little bundle away from her and held it up
against the light. Can you see? She lifted her eyes and looked up
to the light and some of the hairs glinted bright against the dying sun. You see he said, another redhead.

That is enough she cried upon him. I have had enough. You
are a hypocrite! she shouted upon him. You know who I am and
you keep me here to protect your spleen. Her eyes sprang out at
him and forced him back. Do you hear me, I hate and loathe
you, I have found you out, hypocrite and liar that you are. She
shook like a poplar in the wind. I am Jesus Christ and will
avenge your betrayal.

I think I had better go he said. I wish you would be careful.
Youve been so much better lately. Do you hear what I say? she
shouted at him again. I see it all, I know you now. She stood
away from him and her face urged forward. You want my child,
you want my life. I see through your eyes to your little meagre
soul. You are cruel and you want me to stay away from you so
you can borrow the doctor's books. I wet my hair in the tub for
you she cried passionately, and you did not come.

He went away. She saw him go, back to the Day Room and through and past the ferns to the door beyond. He asked a nurse to open for him and he passed out to the doctor's office. She saw him go, she saw the light fade slowly through the trees. She turned her face to the window pane and hot sluices were prepared upon her cheeks for the gold to run down molten. It dropped upon her knees and went back into the fading sun.

XVIII

Dr Brainerd called her aside when she was making her rounds. I hear you dont like Mrs Glope she said.

I was thinking of sending you both over to the West Side said Dr Brainerd. Well said Marthe, I suppose I could stand it for the chance of getting there. Then I am going home soon? she cried clasping and unclasping her hands. You were very funny at the meeting said Dr Brainerd. You took us by surprise. Whats all this youve said to your husband? she said. Do you really object to my lending him my books? She seemed embarrassed.

Ryerson came to get her. All her things were packed. She could not find the letter from her father nor could she find her new tube of cold cream. It had been given to Miss Wade and was not in the drawer. Let those things go said Ryerson, you can get them later. No said Marthe, I am never coming up here again. I want that letter from my father.

Miss Wade had thrown away the letter because it was left on a chair. The cold cream was found in Miss Wade's private drawer, crumpled and used. You used my cream, you didnt ask me. What do you mean, with rounded eyes, you used it yourself.

I wont forget these things. She threw away my father's letter to the end.

She took her clothes, tied in the wide soft kimono, and walked with Ryerson over to the West Side. Goodbye Miss Wade. Goodbye Mrs Gail, white glazed frosting.

Down through the Day Room and past the figures there. Youll see them at meals, you neednt say goodbye. Down the little corridor where she had sat with Christopher and told him not to come. Now the West Side, palms and leather chairs. Upstairs for you. They climbed the stairs and Ryerson opened one of the doors.

She had a room, she was to be alone. Now she knew she must be well, she wanted to be alone. Darling Ryerson how are you coming with Charley? Hes got a cold said Ryerson.

The room was small and the bed had a white coverlet. A bureau and two chairs and a rug on the floor. She could turn on the light herself and put it over the bed. Ryerson left her and she put all her things carefully in the drawers and her father's picture on the bureau. Ryerson came back with a package. This is for you, your husband left it with the doctor. It was wrapped in brown paper and tied up with cord.

She opened and found the black notebook with all the poems in it. And there was a large packet of letters addressed to Christopher, all of them slashed open. On the top one Christopher had written, Read these and cheer up. She sat and read all of the letters. They all told him how sad it was. They all said what a splendid mind she had had. She wept to read their sadness. There were four books besides and her fountain pen. A knock came at the door. She rebelled. Going to open it she saw Miss Baird. She flung her arms about Miss Baird and hugged her soft and pliant warmth. I didnt know it was you. They sat by the window and looked out on the snow. You can see my porch said Miss Baird, its just around the corner. Automobiles skimming past in the road beyond. It doesnt seem like the same place does it? The bars said Marthe, dont you see, the bars are not broken down.

What is this book? Miss Baird fingered and opened tentatively the black leather notebook. O give that back to me, give it back do you hear? She seized it from her hands. They talked until the dark had come. I wonder what is the matter with Miss Baird, she is perfectly well, why does she stay here?

She went to sleep peacefully that night in her new room. The morning came and she dressed early and was ready for the exercises after breakfast. When can I stay afterwards and wash the dishes? Why cant I stay when I want to and they dont? No said little Mrs Mills, you have to be quiet. They let her carry trays to the West Side and she walked carefully down the hall and through the Day Room. The trays were for the surgical patients. They had different food, that was from the diet kitchen.

You can have that egg, I dont want it. A very pretty lady in bed with arthritis had four half-grown children who came to see her. My daughter is ashamed to come and see me. I remember I remember very well said Marthe. Do the doctors say how much she looks like you? Yes said the woman. How did you know? I remember said Marthe, when I went with my father.

The exercises, they said she was to go. Miss Baird came at half past nine and they went in a group through the dining room and down the corridor past the kitchen. Thats where the Conference was. Around the corner and down another hall to a pair of gray doors. The nurse swung out her chain of keys and pulled the great door open.

It was bright and bewildering, a great light room and all around in chairs sat men in coloured shirts. It smelled like a smoking barnyard. There was a green table and two men were walking slowly around it with sticks. Some were standing talking. She looked to the side and there was another room, longer than the first and filled with beds set end on end, beds in long lines and white men in them all. She glanced away and back again and saw these people in their beds white and deserted and most of them with moustaches on their faces. They stared and stared at her, they stared at her eyes and at her legs. There was nothing else, only beds and the white men in them, close packed in the room with space to walk between the rows.

Whats the matter with them? Theyre bedridden the nurse said.

Through this and the gaping eyes behind her legs and up a long and square-turning stairway beyond, grated in. At the top the nurse put in another key and the grated door swung to and they passed within and it snapped behind them. Straight away she saw Mary who was sitting on the floor leaning her face against the grating and looking downstairs. She rushed to her. Is this where you are now?

I am up here, when they get up here they stay.

She took her arm and they went into the big room at the left. There seemed to be a hundred women there and they made chirping noises and moved about restlessly and talked to themselves and to the ceiling. I must be perfectly well ordered. The women sang and walked about. They wore checked dresses and aprons except for some who had on better clothes. They were old, and their faces were eating into their lives. Someone was ironing with a cold iron and it was Annabel. Her cheeks were pink and her ribbon was scarlet. I am ironing this dress for your baby. She would not talk to Marthe.

Someone majestic went sailing up the room to the piano stool and sat with nose glasses and a knot of hair into the piano, regarding the music. It was Miss Ewing. Miss Ewing received all the relatives and was thoughtful of their needs. Everyone spoke of her and how no one could take her place. She sat at a desk in the reception hall and smiled and bowed people in and out, the doctor is busy just this minute isnt there something I can do?

A nurse stood at the head of the room and clapped her hands. Gradually they formed in a line and straggled around the room. The rest sat down in the chairs and chortled at the others. They were formed in a line and the music struck up and they marched around the room. Marthe marched like a drum major, the nurse said when she passed, She must have had gymnastic training.

They formed in broken lines for the drill and nurses stood at the sides to keep them straight. Letty was in front of Marthe and shot her fat hips from side to side to mock the nurse at the head. Some of those in the lines stood still and looked around and some did tardily what was commanded. Some of them laughed at Letty and when they marched around again to the same music there was a group of doctors standing in the door-way watching them. Letty made grimaces at the nurse and shook her ears and spoiled the line.

As soon as it was over the nurse took them back again. Cant I stay with Mary and Annabel? No you have to go back. She clung to Mary's hand. Come along come along cried the nurse. She went downstairs looking up at the shouting and grimacing. I will come back tomorrow she called back up to Mary.

Now she knew that all that was needed was for her to have done every piece of work that was to be done there, and when she had completed every one and answered all the questions correctly she could go home. It would be known then, God would be known. She would be free and able to take things in her own hands and do as it had been ordered.

She cleaned and sang and cleaned, and ferreted out her life. She took the brooms away from those who were sweeping and the floor oiler from the nurse who was doing the Day Room. Resistance that was to be expected there would always be someone who would try to impede her. The woman who did the West Side bathroom was angry with her and said she should not have been allowed there but she prevailed in the end and cleaned every portion of it. She cleaned out the room where the baths were (now three times a week at seven o'clock she could have baths in the shower room where her rings had been taken) and moved the cases and found dirt behind and things that had been lost for many months. The redhaired one glared fiercely at her because she found a pack of cards she had hidden there, and Miss Baird and Letty and Miss Onions played in the afternoon after that. Miss Onions had been there for five years and was on the West Side now. She did the room where the tubs stood for the prolonged baths, and sang for the occupants who yelled for her to stop. One of them was Mary. Mary was back again in East Hall and she was in the tub now showing her dimple. Her hair was short and jagged, she had done it with the scissors. She had white teeth and Marthe fed her lunch. I love you I wish you would get on well and come on the West Side. Mary told her about her lovers and what they had done. She was a maid in a rich family. I havent had any kids. Dont have any said Marthe, they will never let you see them if you do. Mary said she was seventeen.

I dont want to play bridge, I have hated it all my life.

They played in the Day Room in the afternoon and Marthe could not remember the cards. You are the limit, cant you keep your mind on the game? She was always looking away and thinking of something else. They wouldnt play any more. One afternoon when they were trying to put up with her, because Miss Onions was a fine bridge player and played seriously for buttons, a stretcher with a large person covered up was brought in rapidly across the room and carried into East Hall. Thats Mrs Wolf again said Miss Baird, and stopped playing. She looked at Miss Onions. I suppose its the same thing.

Miss Macauley came over to them. She got outrageously drunk last night in the Olympia Theatre she said, and screamed and made an awful row. It took three policemen to bring her in. Shes such a fine woman said Miss Baird, and shook her head. I suppose she'll get six months this time.

Mrs Wolf's son was standing by the desk waiting for the doctor to come. He was in a blue uniform and had his cap in his hand. He was small and thin and shrunken. Marthe looked at his wormeaten face. Too bad said Miss Onions, hes such a nice young man and has a good position. Its your deal she said. Hes always tried to help her said Miss Baird, think what a life hes had.

Marthe looked across at him again to see his face. He was standing by the desk watching them. She left the game and went over to him and timidly took his arm. He gave her a frightened look and drew quickly away from her, backing himself up against the wall, and white. He moved along the wall nearer the desk and held out his arm. She wont hurt you said Miss Macauley.

The baby and the mother. White frozen bitterness. She went and closed her door.

The next afternoon a huge gaudy woman with flashing earrings came out from East Hall and smiling at the nurses sat down poisedly on the sofa in the Day Room. Miss Baird went up to her at once and shook her hand and Miss Onions sat beside her and they talked. The woman had clear eyes and her mouth was easy. I think they are right, she is an interesting woman.

They played bridge again, without Marthe who sat reading by the window. They played with the redhaired one Miss Vaughan who always turned away from Marthe. It was after the sewing. She had refused to sew anything more complicated than rags. The Occupational Therapy woman who came every afternoon at two had said she was to do rags because she would have to do something. She went into East Hall after that to iron some handkerchiefs and Brunmark's cuffs. I bet you wouldnt iron anything for me. I'll fool you, I will do it for you.

In East Hall she visited around. She threw a pillow hard at the skeleton's head to make her stop shouting. When she had finished sitting on the pillow the skeleton's yellow cheeks were pink and she gasped and cursed into the ward. You see said Luella, you got a rise out of her. Youd better not get any more rises said Brunmark, if you want to stay on the West Side. Did you think I wasnt going to get off the pillow? I just wanted to shut her up for one minute. Youd better shut yourself up first said Brunmark. Did you hear the words she said to me? said Marthe. Dr Halloway says she used to be the primmest old maid that ever lived, she lived next door to her. They lose some of that when they get in here said Brunmark.

She liked the ironing. Smooth and out every wrinkle, hard press and forward down and through the cloth. Out and stiff and white and Brunmark's cuffs. She sang to the folding. She looked up once and there was Miss Weinschenck coming in softly looking at her as before. Her pimpled face in the moon.

How do you do she said and held the scorching iron back on her wrist with a movement of her wrist. Miss Weinschenck retreated smiling cold and Marthe gave back the cuffs to Brunmark and went out the opened door. I am not afraid of them I am not like Miss Onions rushing in to iron with holding breath and keeping shut the door.

Mrs Glope was a nuisance, she took her bath and would not wash. I have to stand and wait for her and she doesnt do a thing but fold her towels. Why do I have to wait? You mustnt be so selfish they said.

She was alone now and in her room. She would clean until exhausted and then go to her room and read. The nurses were in a conspiracy to keep her from cleaning. Youll get too tired. It isnt that, I know it is to keep me from finding out the truth so I can go home.

The morning after she was dusting the piano in the fern room when Mrs Wolf went by. Dr Brainerd was with her and two nurses. She heard Mrs Wolf laugh as the door was opened which would let her through and upstairs to Ward 33 where she would remain six months. Its all the same to me, the people here are as good as they are outside. Marthe remembered the large strong figure of Mrs Wolf looming back and laughing from her rouge and talking familiarly in a deep voice to the nurses as she went upstairs for six months.

XIX

Miss Macauley white and smiling trimly was going to take her for a walk beyond the bars. Dr Brainerd had said she could go. Dr Brainerd had been there for twenty years.

Marthe waited in her blue coat with the gray wolf collar and cuffs. It was the first time she had worn it. She had lent it to Miss Lanier to go out on the porch but she had not been allowed on the porch herself. Miss Lanier sat shivering in it in a chair with rubbers and an elderly hat. Wheres your hat? said Miss Macauley dressed in brown, pretty over her uniform. She could not find it and she had to wear someone else's hat.

They went out the side door from the West Side. It opened naturally. Will you do one thing for me? Will you leave your keys behind? Miss Macauley went back and put her keys in her desk. Another nurse unlocked the door for them again.

They stepped out upon the icy walk, sluicing into rivulets in the sun. The grass was brown and mushy and stunk of spring. Close to the low brick buildings were blackened shrubs, cut low and dead of life. She looked intensely at them and not the faintest green. It is the fifth of March.

The air was warm except for the wind which whipped their legs and they chose to go up the road to the left. They looked out at the sun which went into a mist from time to time. They thrust their bare hands into the pockets of their warm coats and swung against the wind. I love the outdoors said Miss Macauley. They flared up the road with measured gait, breathing deep the balanced air and tramping down the little snow that was left on the drying walk. By the side of the walk rose up the bare branches of trees, the trunks sopping and glistening through the sun. Pads of soaked leaves sunk by the road, brown and ruddy and deep in mire. Be careful of the mud, you should have worn your rubbers.

Marthe did not speak. Out beyond them spread brown fields and in the very distance a horse was loping, a woman on his back. She looked with anger. I'll never ride again. Swift rising to the neck and legs bent surely to the flanks. Mounting with grace of adder the sweet swinging stirrups in the spring, and off and out beyond through mud and sunken leaves. Down galloping hair to the wind and hugging with fearful clutch the mane, while clotting hoofs spread pebbles to the sky and eyes swam the trees until the moon was gone. The black and trodden leaves give pungent breath into my nostrils; in its quiet girth thus, with my senses taut, to make my death.

Weve got to turn around, theres the superintendent's house. Dr Armitage? No hes the assistant, thats where Dr Greene lives. They had come to the end of the walk, and muddy road stretched beyond thick and deep. O let me put my feet in it just once. No, no you mustnt. I dont know what I was thinking of to let you come out without your rubbers.

The large pleasant brick house with green trimmings stood stark on the edge of the woods beyond. There were trees and mud and buried leaves. Sunlight and snow and storm.

They turned around and started back. You are getting so much better, youll surely go home before another month. Month, another month? You havent been here very long you know. The sun was gone into the sky, and wearily the trees sagged across the road.

Tell me is there any chance that I shall have to come back here again? Dr Brainerd thinks not. Even if I had another child? No. But I have no child, he is dead. Your child is not dead Mrs Gail.

Would you like to go to the store before we go in? Down there? You can buy fruit and crackers if you like, I'll lend you the money. They went cautiously across the muddy road and down the other side, past a cheap row of houses and a little store on the corner with groceries and chewing gum and candy.

What do you want? said Miss Macauley. Marthe dazed looked about her, boxes high with crackers, glittering things laid out to see, coloured of many kinds. A man and woman came into the store to buy something and stood and stared at her. The woman whispered to the man and they looked again.

Her cheeks grew warm and over all her body flushed the shame. She looked at Miss Macauley, there was her uniform below her dress and cuffs below her sleeves. I want some lollypops she said calmly.

All the way back she thought of that and her face became again scarlet and white. Why dont you suck your lollypop? Im going to give them out in East Hall.

That night was Mrs Glope sweeping down the corridor in her purple dress. I am going to report you to the doctors. The hell I care she told her. She had found Mrs Glope in her room looking at her father's picture and had pushed her out. I shall report you said Mrs Glope, and you wont be allowed to go to the party. The next day Dr Halloway was in the Day Room, Mrs Glope talked grandly to her and turned her back on Marthe. Marthe referred to New York State Underwear.

It was Sunday and Dr Halloway sent for Dr Brainerd and they spent an hour laughing in the chairs. Well said Dr Brainerd, I shall have to go. She sighed and thumped her hand upon the arm of her chair. I hope you two will learn to be friends. Its too bad when you have to see so much of each other. She looked at Dr Halloway and burst into a laugh.

My dear Dr Brainerd said Mrs Glope, please remember that I come from well bred people. She walked away. The doctors were let out at the far door.

It was very cold and she was out on Miss Baird's porch for the day. She was soundly wrapped in woollen things, her feet in sheepskin slippers. Miss Baird had tucked her in with blankets, under the sheets, under the wind and the snow. She gazed out at the trees through the wire grating and went warmly to sleep in the wind.

She came softly and lazily out of the heavy slumber and a dream and back to it again and out again blinking to the glitter of sinking sun across the trees. There on a chair beside the bed was a tray with dinner mouldy and dry that had been standing all afternoon. It must be five o'clock. She turned her freshened cheeks to the wind that carried crystal of snow across the porch, and sank again into the dream.

She hunched her shoulders down under the blankets and her nose without. The cold wind snapped the trees and the sun went down behind the bars. I dont want to get up, I am never going to get up. She lay and dozed and the white wind whistled her frost-nipped nose.

After a while the door began to rock, stamping against it to open it, and Miss Ryerson on the porch. Your husband is downstairs. Send him up here, will they let him come up here? Her small face swallowed in pillows and blankets. Im down in East Hall said Ryerson, now Brunmarks gone over to 33. She took the tray back down with her.

He sat in the chair by the side of the bed and planned her coming home. You wont do a thing for a month and you shall have your son. She put her hand outside of the bed and gripped his hand. Darling if you will only believe me he said, I am so tired waiting for you. They looked at each other for a long time.

She went down to her room with him, dragging blankets, and got dressed. He turned away from her while she was dressing. They sat in her room until the darkness had fallen and the lights glittered across the road. Down the valley from the heights they glittered, a whole city, and out to the bay, and the cloud from the train went fuming by when it whistled around the bend.

The supper bell rang and he must go. She held to him. She kissed quietly the sleeve of his coat. They went downstairs to the Day Room.

A scuffling and muffled shout from the foot of the stairs leading up to the dormitory. She ran, and Miss Baird in a ring of nurses pounding them with her fists and leaning back upon them fainting. She struck out fiercely and with face of pain leaned back and dropped her head. Her face grew into smiles and then in contortions of dismay, and again she struck out with delight and tried to squeeze their necks. They held her arms, they held her wrists, and her face was light and peace. They took her ecstatic to East Hall, and came back from the swung locked door.

Miss Baird is sick again it was said. After supper she took the book and went in past the key into East Hall.

Miss Baird was lying in bed in the room that she herself had had for all that time, the room where there had been the death. She was quiet when Marthe came in. I thought you would come. I came to read to you said Marthe.

She read aloud from the book and Miss Baird listened in the night. There was no light in the room and Marthe had to stand out in the hall under the red glimmer and read through the open door. Ryerson shifted to Godwin while she read and Godwin patted her going by. Why Godwin youve bobbed your hair, you cannot frighten me any more.

They are beautiful said Miss Baird, and I want you to read the rest tomorrow. Will you be back on the West Side tomorrow? Marthe said. I dont know said Miss Baird, sometimes I go right back and sometimes I get transferred. Do you want me to rub your forehead the way you used to do to me when I was in the sheet? No said Miss Baird, I think you had better go to bed.

She went out in the hall and talked to Godwin. The night voices had begun calling to each other across the lights. Where is Kemp, has she gone? Didnt you hear, Kemp tried to escape this afternoon. Shes been taken over to the Main Building. What did she do? She ran away from Wright and out the open door? In the snow? Yes right after she had been in the tub. Its lucky she didnt catch her death. Did they get her, where? She only had on a bathrobe and she ran clear around the building and out in the front. She scared the visitors half to death.

When she had climbed the fire escape from the green swing and saw the woman sitting on the bed with the slinking braids and the square mouth retching.

People escaped sometimes. Miss Baird had told her once of a woman, now gone to the Main Building, who had escaped without anyone's seeing and hid for days under a bench in a park until a policeman found her. You have to stay much longer after that, it was like prison. The prison was on the other side of them, it was up the road to the right beyond the Main Building.

It was long and red, they said, it was the county penitentiary. Between the bughouse and the jail, the motorists used to say, going down Keyser's Road on summer nights.

The woman got away. She ran from the keys and the grating and the bars and under a green bench she jerked her head till four fat policemen found her.

XX

You want to go to the movies this afternoon? had been asked
around and a small dozen was collected. Marthe had not heard
before of movies and said she would go. Out and above the dull
rattling down the halls, after the coats had been pushed on, was
the argument at the door. The tall blonde young woman, who
had tried to transfer her gold wedding ring to Marthe upstairs
when they were making valentines, was walking very fast behind
the nurse. At the door she ceased with gritted lips and turned
upon her heel. Come on we're late said Maude the nurse, the
fragile stray-haired one who kept the clothes. The young
woman tossed her head and remained standing. Her green-
yellow hair was in a dropping knot. Her hands roved over the
large brown buttons of her coat and her eyes opened and closed
in dull resistance. The rest lagged expectant.

Come on said Miss Maude, and urged her arm. She struck
Miss Maude impotently on the shoulder. There said Maude, I
said she shouldnt have been allowed to go. She crooked her arm
about the young woman's neck forcing upward her head. She
did it awkwardly. (Some day youll get hurt, you dont know
enough to take care of yourself.) Are you going to behave now?
The others waited until she had found another nurse to take the
girl back to her ward.

The doors clanged open, richest winter air. Flight of white
snakes in dizziest mountain springs, and over all the breath of
frozen snow. They plunged out into the frost and went carefully
down the slippery walk.

It was in this outdoors, it was again the trees and unbreathed
air. They picked across the muddy road past the brick buildings.
A gang of men in mufflers and large caps came by and flirted
shovels after them. Behind them shouted a man nurse, and it

was Mills. (He is not kind to Mills and her child lives away from her.) He was a vain and selfish head. He set his pettish mouth and said, Get on, you! to the men.

They went up the long flight of steps and into one of the hospital buildings. On the stairs an Italian woman was laughing, crying as she descended, and stopping to laugh. They went gravely up, and up to the top and through a swinging door. Now to find seats, Maude nervously keeping them together. I can depend on you Mrs Gail, stay there and watch Miss Ferris.

Marthe darted her eyes about the great dark hall where many white faces turned eyes inward. She sat in the stiff chair holding Miss Ferris' hand and looking at the screen. People were running, a large gathering crowd, pursuing a serious fellow who was eluding them by jumping over fences. He fled before a trolley car and all the crowd fled after him.

There were lonely chuckles here and there in the profound and deafening silence. Dully they sat and stared, and frozenly they stalked their heads and murmured to themselves. In this great gathering of men and women on a winter's Saturday afternoon, when the heavy walls sweated the stillness and the breathing of his fellow was next to every man, there was a bed of sand along the sea, of sand unrolled and swept upon, left bled and vacant by the tide.

The hero of the picture thrust his thumb into the cap of a milk bottle and a spout of cream sprang up into his eye. Miss Maude bent over with trembling shoulders and a dozen riotous laughs broke loose from the tight-lipped crowd. The rest stared guiltily on, waiting for the moment when their nurses should take them home, and some fixed their eyes upon their knees and made patterns of their handkerchiefs.

The picture changed. Marthe looked with outstretched eyes, adjusting slowly her senses to the scene. There swelled from about the walls and the floor great dripping waxen candle ends gone dry with stale neglect, and become a moist and seething smell. A serpent-toothed torment droned from the hot set minds and covered the close cropped heads with devilled discontent. From the windows, high and darkened by the sacks of brown despair, poured down upon their drooling mouths a mist, heavy with wind-conceived duress.

It will not ever change from this. They will always stare, deathheads rattling in a Bluebeard closet, knotting their sandy handkerchiefs and leaning forward to their feet to spit their prey.

Her eyes piled with broken drops. I am the Christ and cannot do for them.

Their featureless flatness, gray indifference, came all at once to a bright spring of water, white relief of barren trees. There was a rumbling of little thunder in the west, came lightly, softly loudening in the air, the ceiling reaching, to return and burst upon a shower. The great hall shook with mirth, redoubled and reshook and pounded on the floor.

She looked fast at the screen and a house was burning, clever lapping flames licking the fragile frame. About to crash, about to fall within. The hero was returning lost, his love within the flames. They laughed, they screamed, their heads lopped from shoulder to shoulder and their bright eyes shot out and quivered snakes' tongues of delight. They mashed their hands upon the seats and their feet on the wooden floor and cried, The flames! the flames!

The hero made a third dash into the burning house and staggered forth again, his love upon his shoulders hanging limp. Just out, and a crash of burning timbers falling, and all the house came roaring down upon the spot where he had lately fled. Their eyes, ignited with the flames, passed with the flames into an ember, and became again soft ashes finely sifted.

Come on said Maude, help me get these back home again. They went down the long stairs withering, in small groups huddling, until outside, when Maude hurried them across the melted muck and back to the other building.

Into the stale and stifling air again, and clanged the door. Down the long corridors and through the locked doors they filed in dull return, back through the dining room and past the tables crumpily set for the meal. Through the door and past the ferns and into the Day Room where those who had not gone sat dreamily staring and murmuring in little groups. And back and up the stairs, the long and heavy flight that went up miles into oblivion, once to release and now again to flame.

There said Maude to Miss Wade, here they are. She stayed and told about the movie and the figures went slowly back to their sentinel posts and sat. Miss Maude and Miss Wade in conversation standing at the door. And they got married? O yes said Maude, there was the wedding and everything. Next week theyre going to show Jack Gordon in The Denuded Woman. I think I'll go said Wade.

XXI

She wandered listlessly about after breakfast with a half-read
book in her hand. They would not let her work any more.
You get too tired. She had been allowed to stay behind the
others after supper and she had washed great piles of plates
and wiped more piles. She had darted up and down the long
corridor outside the kitchen with the dish wagon, she had
polished a million spoons. That morning she was told that it
was finished. She would not be allowed to work again. They
are always stopping me, they think I dont know its to keep me
from going home. She did not sleep in the night. She came
trailing down to Miss Sheehan's desk in the early morning to
tell her to look into the papers. She said she would see
Christopher's suicide.

Where are you going with that tray, is there someone in the
tubs this time of day? She was going to iron her clothes. Its for
Mary Soulier. Is she down here now? Yes shes in the Strong
Room. What, the Strong Room! Marthe followed Ryerson in.
She had seen the Strong Room once before when a new patient
was being admitted to it, a dark foreign girl, giddy, whose arm
she had held to keep her from striking Dr Brainerd.

Ryerson opened the door while Marthe held the tray. There
was Mary Soulier in the bed in her little nightgown with all the
covers on the floor. Youll have to have the sheet said Ryerson,
youll catch your death in here. Hello said Mary, are you going
to stay? Let me feed her. Look out she doesnt bite you said the
nurse.

The room was small and lighted by a little window at the top.
It was absolutely bare except for the bed, which had iron legs
clamped to the floor. Its cold in here said Marthe. There isnt
any heat said Mary, they told me I wouldnt have to stay if I

would behave, but I kept right on. What have you been doing? I hate them said Mary.

She put the covers back over her and tucked her in. Mary's face was round and looked up smiling like a child. Havent you got anything to brush your hair with first? No not in the Strong Room. She pulled a strand of her wild hair across her nose and made a face. You certainly did make a mess of your hair said Marthe to her, what on earth possessed you to do that? Well theyll never give you any scissors for fear youll do something, so I thought Id give them something to think about. As if they cared said Marthe. Your lovely soft hair. Dr Brainerd cared said Mary, she said she always liked my hair.

Well are you going to eat? She put the tray down on Mary's lap and sat on the foot of the bed. Mary picked at the breakfast and talked. Her face twitched and grimaced. She told all of her life and all the byways. I dont mind it here she said, Mrs Grosvenor sends me oranges from Florida. She had been a maid in a rich household before coming there. My mother comes and cries, the silly old bitch. Dont you like her? What she has done for me said Mary. Shes an awful old liar and Dr Brainerd believes her. Dont fool yourself said Marthe, Dr Brainerd does not believe anyone.

Now I have got to go and take your tray. Dont go cried Mary, and seized her dress. She kissed the skirt. I like you, I dont want you to go. But I cant stay here, I have to iron. Mary frowned and stared her eyes and gritted her teeth. You are not going to leave me! She leaped into the air and clawed the bedclothes. She seized upon Marthe's shoulders and glared into her face. I will kill you if you leave me.

Marthe held her arms. Imagine putting you in the Strong Room. I suppose up there in 33 you terrified them all she said. You really do look pretty dreadful. Like a thunder cloud come out of the west. Im taking care to hold you hard because they say that you can bite.

Youre goddamned right I can, and if you try to go I'll bite you so you wont forget it.

Marthe backed around, holding still to her wrists. She backed against the door and called through the panel. Youre a fool she said. I'll never come again.

Limp to the floor went Mary in a lump and began to weep her shoes. Its all right, here comes the nurse. Ryerson clanged open. What do you mean by letting this door shut? do you want to get killed in here alone with that demon?

I'll come to see you again Mary she said. The radiant smile saddened her face. She got back quickly into the bed.

Marthe went with Ryerson back through the Day Room and into East Hall. I have got to iron. She went around to the beds to visit, and into the rooms, and returned to the little room at the head of the hall where Mrs Welsh had been ironing and singing long ago on the other side of Marthe's wall.

She was singing high and keen when Ryerson came running and pushed open the door. Shes after me she gasped, help me if you can, shes afraid of you. Fast behind Ryerson came Luella, her kinky hair starting out and her pugnosed mouth set in sullen anger. Here here cried Marthe, what are you doing Luella, let go of her. She dropped her iron and came between. I'll get her, never mind.

Ryerson went shaking against the wall and Marthe pushed Luella tightly out the door. Shes strong, I dont know if I can hold her. They clinched and down upon the floor they both went rolling, and Ryerson came to, and back to help. Stay out of this said Marthe, get the sheet and I'll get her to her bed.

Slowly the hands came round her throat to squeeze her to obey. Luella aroused, and stubbornly she put out of her way what bothered her to get at Ryerson. Marthe struck out and in the blaze of coming rigidly down upon Luella's head she got away and stood up above her. She leaned and took two full clutches of her strong thick hair and began to pull her to her bed.

Luella with a powerful wrench (Ryerson's white cheeks on the sides) shook off the hands and struck at Marthe's face. White moons again and this time it would be for herself. The door came wide and Letty and a nurse. Look at this Gail rowing again can you beat that? bawled Letty. She hurled herself into the fray and tugged at Marthe's hair.

You get out of this, this is none of your damned business.

Ryerson had come and was explaining to the nurse. They held Luella and walked her stiffly back to her bed and put the sheet.

You little devil, who told you to pull my hair like that, youre too goddamned officious. Help help, screamed fatly from Letty's chin and squeals for help from Letty's stomach. The other nurse came running. Come here said Ryerson, and they bound her arms between them. She'd better go upstairs.

Ryerson held tightly to her arm. Its my fault she whispered, never mind, it will only be a little while and I will tell the doctor it was my fault.

Dr Brainerd is out of the building said Miss Macauley, Gail had better go upstairs until she comes back. They took her upstairs and put her in a room and shut the door. She threw herself on the white bed and streamed her face into the bed.

There had been in sight white gulls swooping over the ship in the early morning and far away to the north and east the gray that meant her long release. And nearer and nearer in the grayness of the morning the ship rolled to the east, where green in the little cranny she had seen the end, the cottages folded into the trees and the great red tank that came to meet the ships.

Now the anchor had been lifted again, and floated out over the choppy seas to waters horridly familiar. Into the pillow went the ship's anchor, and around the ship went whining the bread soaked gulls.

A knock at her door followed by Miss Wade with a tray. I hope Im not going to have you up here again, she said with false offense. She set the tray down on the chair. Keep perfectly quiet and dont you leave this room. She walked out, her smug smile snugly set.

After she had eaten she stared out of the window and sang through the bars to the line of men patients who were on their afternoon parade. She sang the Star Spangled Banner to see if they would lift their hats.

She came softly out of the room and looked to the left. No one at the desk. Down the hall to the far end was Mrs Flynn in her chair. Hello darling said Mrs Flynn, come sit by me theres a dear. In one of the beds was the pale girl. Where have you been all this time? I was in the tuberculosis ward but theyve decided I havent got it.

They were talking energetically when down the floor came Wade and stopped when she came to her. You go straight back to your room, didnt I tell you not to leave it?

It had come, it had come at last, and now it would be cold. She could never get away anyway, she was going all her life to stand behind these bars. She stood up tall and straight against Miss Wade.

You fat smug inefficient little fool she said, whoever gave you authority over so many people who are more decent than you are.

I must not strike her, not hurt her, only humiliate her to the end.

Look here young woman you are not going to talk to me like that. She took hold roughly of her arm. Get right back to your room, you. I know, now I know, Luella taught me what to do.

Miss Wade was forced down upon the floor and made a simple sound. Marthe was sitting across her middle and pushing both hands cunningly about her throat. She will be apt to think that she is dead.

No sound could make Miss Wade from fear, and in the chair Mrs Flynn and in the bed the sallow girl. I hope you are hurting her was all that that girl said and turned away. Mrs Flynn made feeble protest from her chair.

You see you fat and selfsatisfied little humbug you arent magnificent. Here I am above you now and if I choose I can choke the simmering life out of your throat and you wont be able to pull in your accustomed chin. She loosened her hands a moment and Miss Wade's throat contracted to make a feeble scream.

Ive got her down and I am going to kill her said Marthe to Mrs Flynn. I am going to kill her now. She glared into Miss Wade's face and it was white and green.

Came down the hall Miss Harrison and Marthe got up. Miss Wade sprang to her feet and arranged her belt. Take her other side she said, and twisted Marthe's wrist. Marthe flung out and knocked off her cap and was thrown upon the floor by both and dragged by the tight collar of her dress back to the room. She was dragged upon the floor and Miss Harrison opened the door. Miss Wade threw her into the room upon the floor and slammed and locked the door.

When the doctor came she had climbed the grated bars and was hanging with her hands from the top and singing. Get down said Dr Brainerd, I want to talk to you. She climbed down and sat trembling on the bed.

Miss Ryerson says you were trying to help her out. You mustnt help the nurses out. They are capable of taking care of themselves.

Now you are very excited said Dr Brainerd, I think you had better go to sleep. You shouldnt have worked so hard yesterday. You havent been doing anything today have you? I left orders that you were not to do a thing. Why dont you take care of yourself? I thought you were intelligent.

I cant sleep, how can I sleep? I'll give you something, said Dr Brainerd, get undressed.

She went out and returned with Miss Harrison and Miss Wade. I tell you Dr Brainerd, from the bed, you had better not let that woman stay in this room. What have you got against Miss Wade? She had better go out said Marthe fiercely. Go and get Mrs Fenwick said the doctor.

Back came Mrs Fenwick, fat and Irish smiling brown eyes of summer. My darling Fat, and how is Ena? She has a daughter Ena that gets all the prizes at school.

I am going to give you paraldehyde said Dr Brainerd, it will put you to sleep. She took it from Miss Harrison's hand. I want to see my husband, cant I see him today?

No said Dr Brainerd, not today. She held the little glass to Marthe's lips.

Marthe drew back, sputtering the sharpness. I dont like it, please dont make me take it. Yes my dear said Dr Brainerd gently, you must take it now.

I wont, I wont, you cannot make me take it. A sign from the doctor, the two nurses held her jerking arms and legs. She struggled like a fish caught in a net and yearned and stretched her neck to get away. She choked and screamed and turned her body round and kicked her legs and stomach and her throat sprang up and threw back from her the captive stream.

Its down I think and dying, and all that burst was but for me to die. As soon as her mouth was free she turned upon the doctor.

Traitor! she cried upon her there, you my friend, you cruel one, have you never had anyone you cared about kept away from you?

I think I have said Dr Brainerd. She looked with pity and stood off a mountain and a god. You go away from me Marthe impotently cried, dont ever call me friend again. They all went out and locked the door.

I will not go to sleep! she shouted through the grating at the top. I will never sleep!

She got out of the bed and stood by the window, softly dying light. She stood and shivered in the room and her head began to range about. I will not go to sleep, I can keep myself. Her head dropped on her neck and her feet slept beneath her knees. She walked about the room, heavy breath, and stars began to climb. Not now, not now, I will not touch the bed.

Shaking her head again upward to the window she walked herself around the walls and of the floor boards made a ridged parade ground. She drooped and hung down from a stem, and listless rain came down upon her and bent her body to the ground. Leaned and drooped in the rain, and summer rain and marsh, white petals beat into the mud, and dead in the rain gone dead.

Her eyes were closed, her head and shoulders fell across the bed. Into the mud gone dead, and rain and wind of spring.

XXII

They were going to have the party that night.

For weeks they had been planning it and she was to sing an Irish song. Mrs Ivor (who had been in East Hall with the cuts on her face I am a very passionate woman my dear) was also to sing. She had sung in concert and Marthe was afraid she could sing better. Christopher had brought her a new ribbon, bright and blue to wind around her head. Miss MacDougal played the songs while they rehearsed and Dr Walker came in from the other side. His face was white and flabby and he laughed at everything he said. He doesnt seem so dreadful as they say except his teeth.

Dr Walker is the head of the Men's Psychopathic Ward just as Dr Brainerd is the head of the Women's. The entertainment is to be on his service. He is very cruel to the men. Once when the orchestra was rehearsing and Dr Walker was bullying more than usual, the first violin suddenly stood up and cracked him on the head with his violin, breaking it to pieces. He lost his violin and got the Strong Room.

His little girl came with him this time and sat in his lap. He looks so mean, I wonder if he beats his child. They sang and learned the songs, and he said, Everything is ready now and to-night is the party. There were to be entertainers from the town.

After the supper Letty came to her room. What are you going to wear she said. Look at me. Dr Halloway gave me one of her dresses, it was too tight but I let it out. You look very giddy Letty, Im afraid you will disturb those men. Letty's eyes gleamed and she shifted her gum. I expect I will she chortled in her chin. I let Letty out once on trial Dr Brainerd said, and she came back with a baby and a gold watch. I thought Id better keep her after that.

I havent anything to wear except this dress. I have my new ribbon and my shoes are new. Christopher had brought her the shoes. They were black patent leather slippers.

They went round to the other rooms. Miss Baird was not going, she had a headache. Mrs Flynn was in bed. Mrs Glope in dress of purple splendour, her curls laid closely to her forehead, drooped negligently a lace handkerchief. She was ready early. Marthe had seen Annabel and Luella at the exercises in the morning, and knew they would be there. Mrs Welsh could hardly wait, and bounced herself around. Mrs Ivor, elegant in her black low velvet dress, she used to be a movie actress. Her curly hair black and gray and strong goodlooking face. Marthe remembered her naked on the floor, and what a noble body. Come in here said Mrs Ivor. A very passionate woman she had said. Men have been my undoing but I wouldnt change myself. You are the only person here intelligent enough to understand. Of course she said you and I are not made like the rest of them. It is enough for these old maids what they can do alone. Brunmark speaking about the girl who sat next to her at the table and coughed to herself and said thank you. Brunmark said she abused herself. In the tub Brunmark? I guess you dont know much about the inside of a lunatic asylum, Brunmark had retorted.

Everyone was ready and many who did not care to go were urged to go. Marthe was shaking with excitement. She took Letty's hand. The nurse who was to take them across was Miss Albert and she was in charge of the operating room and had iodine on a little cut on her chin.

They were marched across, down all the halls and corridors and through the far door to the great room where the men were. They were sat formally in stiff chairs, in lines. Through the wide swung doors she could see the long hall where all the beds were end on end. They were smoking now, the men nurses watching them. They looked excitedly at the women coming in.

Miss Albert on the end, then Glope, the others and then Letty. Next to Letty Mrs Ivor and Marthe on the far end. When would Luella and Annabel come in from the other side? She watched with vigil eye and when they came all in a bunch and hurried by the nurse, they sat across the room. May I go and see Annabel? Not now said Miss Albert, you will mix later on.

She looked around as groups came in to take their seats. Across from her sat a boy of nineteen with fair hair like her brother's and a drooping head. Next to him a young woman. Thats his sister said Miss Albert in reply. Hes been shell-shocked.

She gazed at the sensitive lips and the indifferent eyes. Then she remembered him, he had been at the movies. Shellshocked, a burst of sound, and all the other bursts were all the same. On the deck going home digging into the splintered deck.

In time it all filled up, and filed in behind them a group of shuffling men. She looked and a bearded Italian was chuckling into his vest. Letty behind arched her smile and tossed her chin at him.

In time Dr Walker the master of ceremonies. First there will be games. Miss Ewing, hair toppling, smiling indulgently at the piano. Into a chord she struck and the nurses all urged upward the lagging feet. They were marshalled into groups and were to swing in folk dances.

In their group was a man who knew the dance very well and would brook no errors. He was long and thin and mustered in his face. You there get back he would say amiably, and the nurse was wrong three-quarters of the time. Marthe found the rhythm of the dance and swung and swayed into its motion. When they danced round in the ring she bent her head and lifted her knees. You be careful said Miss Albert mechanically dont let go of yourself, youre getting excited. She broke angrily out of the dance and went and sat alone in her chair.

When the dancing was over they all sat down. Now said Dr Walker rubbing his oiled hands, we shall have some real dancing. Out of the far hall came fluttering a little girl and boy on spiralled legs and stiff toes, in butterfly and flower costumes. Their faces were plastered down and with steamed smiles they did their pieces. The building stormed applause. I dont understand it seemed to me quite dreadful. They encored and smirked a bow to all the sides of the room. They think they are doing such a favour to us, as if we gave a damn. But the others did, and banged their heels to indicate applause.

Then came out a glib young man with side whiskers half way down, eyebrows and agile knees. A girl in costume of 1830 swept out and they danced a sentimental piece. They make me sick, they have no rhythm in their bodies, he is disgusting, what a face. The house applauded not so hard and after that it was announced that Mrs Isabelle Ivor would sing. My God I will be next.

With presence of one accustomed to public appearance Mrs Ivor stood before the fastened throng and sang contralto depths. They stared and some of them clapped in the middle. Shes through and now will be my turn. She stiffened into the chair. There will be social dancing now said Dr Walker. The orchestra began to play. He has forgotten he has forgotten. She mingled relief with disappointment in the music.

Dr Halloway came up and asked her to dance. She was happy in the dance and Dr Halloway led her smoothly. They plunged into conversation. She is just my age and has some sense. She doesnt treat me like a fool. Isnt he idiotic looking? whispered Dr Halloway. The man dancer with the eyebrows buzzed by with the girl in silk.

WHAT a face said Marthe audibly, and they turned to follow him with their eyes. The man turned too and looked from whirling. What a FACE said Marthe, and turned to stare again. Dr Halloway dissolved into herself and sought a chair. I dont care said Marthe, he thinks we're all crazy so why not take advantage of it to tell him the truth?

She found Luella and Annabel and Mrs Welsh and they talked, and Luella and Annabel were asked to dance. She was standing by Mrs Welsh when the young man went by who was with his sister. His hair was wet and fell across his forehead. He looked straight ahead. Marthe turned to look at him and he stopped and saw her. His sister stopped too. Why dont you ask her to dance? she said to him. Wouldnt you like to dance with him?

Perhaps he doesnt want to said Marthe. The boy stared at Marthe and began to smile in the corners of his mouth. Then he shook his head. No he said. No. He looked again. She has a lovely face he said and sighed.

Why dont you ask her to dance? his sister said again. Youd dance with him wouldnt you, hes a very good dancer. No he said, I cannot dance. He went away from them.

She has a face. A lovely face. My ribbon it must be.

A man with a large chest came by and asked her for a dance. She retreated behind Mrs Welsh. Letty hopped past them spinning her heels and her fat legs upon the floor. She was clutched by a baldhead with red face and sparkling tie pin. She waved to them and gurgled up into his perspiring face.

Mrs Glope came by with lifted nose. Have you been dancing? she observed to Marthe. Very vulgar these men dont you think? I havent seen one who doesnt look like a butcher's apprentice.

Why didnt you invite the greatest ornithologist in the State of New York? How silly of you said Mrs Glope, do you suppose my son could spare the time for this? I am going to bed.

If James were only here called Marthe after her, he would certainly dance with me. Do you suppose he has no taste at all? she twisted back and sniffed.

The nurses collected their groups and counted. Come on said Miss Albert, youll see her again another time. Marthe was dragged from Annabel and out the door they went, she looking back to see again the long hall and all the beds and the hunched up legs under the spreads.

XXIII

She was at the piano one afternoon and Christopher had not come. I want him so. I want my husband she said to Miss Macauley going by. You must learn to control that, all the married women have to. What does she mean, whatever does she mean?

Later some visitors came in and wanted to see someone. They sat and waited while Marthe went to find Miss Macauley. When she came back Marthe found them laughing together looking at Mrs Teale who was walking in a circle.

Youd better not laugh at her said Marthe, we're all crazy here and some of us are wild. The visitors looked abashed and sat with strained faces.

She was in her room and put her books together. I wonder if I am ever going home. She told me I had no delusions left. She doesnt know of course.

You of sternmouthed penitence, guard well my silver shoes. You reached and stole them from the morning and some day when water lilies hang at your door in a prim wicker basket I shall buy shoes of dull black and shimmer them with imitation silver.

Visitors for you Mrs Gail.

She went below and there were Margaret Stein and Jane Kittredge with a large pot of flowers. Christopher said we could come to see you.

She sat and talked to them in the dying light. They were curious and she defending. Youll be out soon I know they said in leaving. I wonder if they were afraid.

The next morning she was sitting on the sofa in the Day Room holding yarn for Miss Lanier. Dr Brainerd came down, strong step and vigorous hands. She is so fine, so strong and calm, more God than any god.

How would you like to go home? she said in passing. She started and dropped the yarn. And see my baby's hair.

You can go tomorrow said Dr Brainerd. You will have to go over to the Main Building and get your rings.

In the afternoon she put on her coat and went with Miss Wright to the Main Building. There were the long rows of whitehaired women pale and still (the terminal dementias she said) and the room where they did the weaving. Mrs Kemp, very much thinner, came up to her and pulled her dress. I am going home and she will be here for seven years. I am going out beyond her bars.

They went to the office and Marthe signed a slip and received an envelope containing her rings. She slipped it on, the plain white platinum band and then the little one with the diamond. I dont know why I love them so, I dont like rings. The diamond sputtered in the sun going back, and she had it large upon her finger as she had had it long ago when she had first worn it and went self conscious down the street in the sun. Christopher would come for her tomorrow.

It would be no more for him to come stealing up the walk outside in the snow and rest his feet in the hallway to the doctor's chanting. Christopher, who had seen from the beginning and had brushed from his tears the year's long wait. Christopher who had planned and listened and welded, and to whom she had opened only a field of snow. It had been two months, they said, because there was still the snow.

That had been in green summer and trees and fine-cooled water. He had sat on the bank and puffed and knocked the ashes into the lake. Over the bank and up the hill and down from the pine needles to the water below. Stillness and summer rain. Christopher had been her love.

Alone in her room at night she stood and pressed her face against the window. It was the end of March and had turned cold again. And all the thumbs of ice began to whirl in shaking circles, keeping with the wind. I shall have snow on my glassy fingers she said, and a shutter of snow on my grave tonight.

Trees bold and stiff in the hollow moon, move to the crunch of heels of gold below you. Stars fling past you to ribboned houses beyond. And your hair falls to your feet and hears no wind.

Emily Holmes Coleman was born in Oakland, California, in 1899. She was educated at a private boarding school and then at Wellesley College. She married Lloyd Ring ("Deke") Coleman in 1921, and in 1924 gave birth to a son. Following his birth she suffered puerperal fever, which led to a mental breakdown and a period in Rochester State Hospital in New York—experiences she drew upon for *The Shutter of Snow*.

In 1925 she moved to Paris where she worked as a foreign correspondent for the *Chicago Tribune*, then as secretary to anarchist Emma Goldman. She began publishing her poems in *transition* and became an important figure in the legendary literary life of Paris in the twenties. She moved to London in 1929, and the following year published her only novel. (Another novel, *The Tygon*, remains unpublished.) In the thirties she played a key role in editing and finding a publisher for Djuna Barnes's *Nightwood*.

She returned to America in 1939, and under the influence of Jacques Maritain converted to Catholicism in 1942. Over the next three decades she continued to divide her time between England and America. Her final years were spent in a Catholic worker farm in New York State, where she died in 1974. Throughout her life she kept a diary, which is being edited for publication.

DALKEY ARCHIVE PAPERBACKS

FELIPE ALFAU, *Locos.*
    Sentimental Songs.
ALAN ANSEN,
    Contact Highs: Selected Poems 1957-1987.
DJUNA BARNES, *Ladies Almanack.*
    Ryder.
JOHN BARTH, *LETTERS.*
    Sabbatical.
ROGER BOYLAN, *Killoyle.*
CHRISTINE BROOKE-ROSE, *Amalgamemnon.*
GERALD BURNS, *Shorter Poems.*
MICHEL BUTOR,
    Portrait of the Artist as a Young Ape.
JULIETA CAMPOS, *The Fear of Losing Eurydice.*
LOUIS-FERDINAND CÉLINE, *Castle to Castle.*
    North.
    Rigadoon.
HUGO CHARTERIS, *The Tide Is Right.*
JEROME CHARYN, *The Tar Baby.*
EMILY COLEMAN, *The Shutter of Snow.*
ROBERT COOVER, *A Night at the Movies.*
STANLEY CRAWFORD,
    Some Instructions to my Wife.
RENÉ CREVEL, *Putting My Foot in It.*
RALPH CUSACK, *Cadenza.*
SUSAN DAITCH, *Storytown.*
COLEMAN DOWELL, *Island People.*
    Too Much Flesh and Jabez.
RIKKI DUCORNET, *The Fountains of Neptune.*
    The Jade Cabinet.
    Phosphor in Dreamland.
    The Stain.
WILLIAM EASTLAKE, *Lyric of the Circle Heart.*
ANNIE ERNAUX, *Cleaned Out.*
LAUREN FAIRBANKS, *Muzzle Thyself.*
    Sister Carrie.
LESLIE A. FIEDLER,
    Love and Death in the American Novel.
RONALD FIRBANK, *Complete Short Stories.*

FORD MADOX FORD, *The March of Literature.*
JANICE GALLOWAY, *Foreign Parts.*
    The Trick Is to Keep Breathing.
WILLIAM H. GASS,
    Willie Masters' Lonesome Wife.
C. S. GISCOMBE, *Here.*
KAREN ELIZABETH GORDON, *The Red Shoes.*
GEOFFREY GREEN, ET AL, *The Vineland Papers.*
PATRICK GRAINVILLE, *The Cave of Heaven.*
JOHN HAWKES, *Whistlejacket.*
ALDOUS HUXLEY, *Antic Hay.*
    Point Counter Point.
EWA KURYLUK, *Century 21.*
OSMAN LINS,
    The Queen of the Prisons of Greece.
ALF MAC LOCHLAINN,
    The Corpus in the Library.
    Out of Focus.
DAVID MARKSON, *Collected Poems.*
    Reader's Block.
    Springer's Progress.
    Wittgenstein's Mistress.
CAROLE MASO, *AVA.*
HARRY MATHEWS, *20 Lines a Day.*
    The Conversions.
    The Journalist.
JOSEPH MCELROY, *Women and Men.*
JAMES MERRILL, *The (Diblos) Notebook.*
STEVEN MILLHAUSER, *The Barnum Museum.*
OLIVE MOORE, *Spleen.*
STEVEN MOORE, *Ronald Firbank: An Annotated*
    Bibliography.
NICHOLAS MOSLEY, *Accident.*
    Assassins.
    Children of Darkness and Light.
    Impossible Object.
    Judith.
    Natalie Natalia.
YVES NAVARRE, *Our Share of Time.*

DALKEY ARCHIVE PAPERBACKS

WILFRIDO D. NOLLEDO, *But for the Lovers.*
FLANN O'BRIEN, *The Dalkey Archive.*
   The Hard Life.
   The Poor Mouth.
FERNANDO DEL PASO, *Palinuro of Mexico.*
RAYMOND QUENEAU, *The Last Days.*
   Pierrot Mon Ami.
REYOUNG, *Unbabbling.*
JULIÁN RÍOS, *Poundemonium.*
JACQUES ROUBAUD,
   The Great Fire of London.
   The Plurality of Worlds of Lewis.
   The Princess Hoppy.
LEON S. ROUDIEZ, *French Fiction Revisited.*
SEVERO SARDUY, *Cobra* and *Maitreya.*
ARNO SCHMIDT, *Collected Stories.*
   Nobodaddy's Children.
JUNE AKERS SEESE,
   Is This What Other Women Feel Too?
   What Waiting Really Means.
VIKTOR SHKLOVSKY, *Theory of Prose.*
CLAUDE SIMON, *The Invitation.*
GILBERT SORRENTINO, *Aberration of Starlight.*
   Imaginative Qualities of Actual Things.
   Mulligan Stew.
   Pack of Lies.
   Splendide-Hôtel.
   Steelwork.
   Under the Shadow.
W. M. SPACKMAN, *The Complete Fiction.*
GERTRUDE STEIN, *The Making of Americans.*
   A Novel of Thank You.
ALEXANDER THEROUX, *The Lollipop Trollops.*
ESTHER TUSQUETS, *Stranded.*
LUISA VALENZUELA, *He Who Searches.*
PAUL WEST,
   Words for a Deaf Daughter and *Gala.*
DOUGLAS WOOLF, *Wall to Wall.*
PHILIP WYLIE, *Generation of Vipers.*

MARGUERITE YOUNG, *Angel in the Forest.*
   Miss MacIntosh, My Darling.
LOUIS ZUKOFSKY, *Collected Fiction.*
SCOTT ZWIREN, *God Head.*

Dalkey Archive Press, ISU Box 4241, Normal, IL 61790–4241
fax (309) 438–7422
Visit our website at www.cas.ilstu.edu/english/dalkey/dalkey.html